PRAISE FOR *HAV*

"What exquisite stories these are   of them immaculately composed, each of them powerfully transporting, carrying us away to Greece and Africa and Toronto and elsewhere, carrying us also into troubled, quietly impassioned human lives that remind us of our own. A superb story is, for me, one that makes me wish I had written it, and I wish I had written all ten of these brilliant, tender, and beautiful stories. This book deserves prizes."

> - Tim O'Brien, author of *The Things They Carried*

"Everybody in this gorgeous, illuminating collection is cheating, posing, yearning, lost—in other words, human. Lisa Cupolo tells these stories with the merciful, merciless third eye of a truly gifted writer."

> - Danzy Senna, author of *Caucasia* and *New People*

"What a remarkable book of stories *Have Mercy on Us* is. With settings that range from small-town Canada to rural Kenya to 1940s Florida, its vibrant plots kept surprising me at every turn. I loved never knowing what these characters were going to do, as the ironies of life unfolded around them. A wonderful collection."

> - Joan Silber, author of *Improvement*, winner of the National Book Critics Circle Award and the PEN/Faulkner Award for Fiction

"Lisa Cupolo has a masterful gift for locating the most vulnerable, make it or break it, moment in a relationship, and then exploring the outcome with great insight and wisdom. The accomplished stories in *Have Mercy on Us*—skillfully varied in tone and geography—come together thematically to reveal the emotional price of love and loss. Will a young mother choose to leave her family? Will a husband continue to cheat even when confronted? Will an unacknowledged child be accepted into a family? Will a child come home when begged to do so? Some of the shifts are subtle but none are simple and all are memorable and satisfying."

— Jill McCorkle, author of *Heiroglyphics*

"In her masterful collection, Lisa Cupolo investigates the tender ironies that define our friendships, marriages and love affairs, our fragile dreams, and the very things that make us human. These heart and soul stories shimmer with intelligence and deep insight, written by a remarkable new voice in fiction."

— Elizabeth Brundage, author of *The Vanishing Point*

"Lisa Cupolo's vivid, earthy, richly imagined stories paint a landscape of legends and losers, well-knit women and trouble-some men, ambivalent mothers and doting fathers—in other words humans at every stage of connection and folly. The mercy in *Have Mercy on Us* is that Cupolo has conjured a world seen through her wise, unflinching, and big-hearted gaze. And that is grace."

— Carol Edgarian, author of *Vera*

HAVE MERCY ON US

J.G. Cupolo

Lisa Cupolo

Regal House Publishing

Published by
Regal House Publishing, LLC
Raleigh, NC 27605
All rights reserved

ISBN -13 (paperback): 9781646033164
ISBN -13 (epub): 9781646033171
Library of Congress Control Number: 2022935699

Cover image and design © by C. B. Royal

Regal House Publishing, LLC
https://regalhousepublishing.com

The following is a work of fiction created by the author. All names,
individuals, characters, places, items, brands, events, etc. were either the
product of the author or were used fictitiously. Any name, place, event,
person, brand, or item, current or past, is entirely coincidental.

Printed in the United States of America

For Richard and Lila

Contents

FELT AND LEFT HAVE THE SAME LETTERS

People knew of us in that small Greek village. The well-known English writer with his family, staying up the hill at the Tourterelle estate, an ancient and sturdy two-story with milky turquoise shutters and fuchsia bougainvillea cascading just so, as if heaven sent. The place was ours for two months' time. May and June.

We were planted and living among the locals.

Anthony had his feet dangling from the open window, pen in hand; he was a bearded man of innumerable and—occasionally—insufferable talents. I remember Louisa came into the kitchen where I was and asked, "Ma, how can I make my skin more luminous?" She wanted something to give her vitality and gloss, she said.

Meanwhile, I was applying clumps of brown henna onto my dwindling strands. "This is the last time," I told my daughter. "Soon I'll go *au naturel*, gray." I was tired of the fuss of dyeing my hair each month. When would I knock off the facade and embrace the years, all the years that stacked up on me sideways like shingles on a roof?

"Start with olive oil," I told my daughter. "Add the pulp of an orange and mash some rosemary in to make a paste, then apply it to your cheeks. Eat a spoonful of raw garlic with honey."

What did I know? Upping the beauty? At her age? Louisa needed not a dash of paint, nor a dab of cover. Youth burst from her lush curls and delighted its way along to her springy toes. A child born under the Lion moon. She was wearing a silk robe that stopped at her tanned thighs.

"Ma," Louisa said, "get the back. Let me do it, eh?" She grabbed the bottle and squeezed the color onto my roots as if it were ketchup she was lining a hot dog with.

Oh, to be young.

You can hear me sigh, can't you?

Once in my own glorious youth, a princely man, not my husband, had professed to me: *My, you have long legs,* he'd said, regarding me up and down.

Yes, I'd told him, *they go all the way up to my ass.* I was full of pluck and vigor then. How else could I have snagged the genius writer?

Louisa was our only one, twenty-six and not a crumb of ambition past her next meal. She claimed to be an *artiste,* but where was the work? Her father had spoiled the be-genius out of her. I'd said this to my cousin who lived in New Jersey. She laughed into the phone and told me that in America twenty-year-olds are all idiots. "Thirty is the new twenty, Daria. You didn't know?" she'd said.

Well, I believed our daughter's dharma would surface soon. "She'll surprise us," I told Anthony. "Maybe after we're gone," I added. "She'll surprise *somebody.*" But you see, my hands were no longer in it, as if I'd clapped the flour dust from them. I brought her into the world. The baton had been passed.

"Done, Ma," Louisa announced. "You're gorgeous," she said, and tossed the brown-stained bottle into the porcelain sink. In truth, our daughter was a kindly person.

It was then that a thick package wrapped in twine was brought to the wooden entranceway by a dirty-faced girl who could have been Lila from Ferrante's Naples. *For Anthony Borland* was written in fanciful cursive. A calligraphic *B.*

"Anthony!" I yelled out the open shutters to the window above, knowing he wouldn't budge. The hair color gnawed at my temples. "A package!" I shifted the towel on my shoulders and went up.

"This came," I said, and held it out. I was ever the servant unto him. Anthony took the package, flipped it over, and then flipped it again. He smiled and set it on the ledge, then picked it up once more. He stood from his writing place and seemed, for that instant, taller and uglier. He might have beaten his chest. Who could say?

He opened the padded envelope and laid out the contents on the wide sill. One by one he examined each item: a diagram, an intricate and beautiful pen drawing, a map, and what appeared to be a numbered list of questions, all directed toward the famous man. Big guffaws of curiosity came out of Anthony's mouth, cavernous sounds. "She's a painter in town," he said, and laughed. "How wonderful. She's ravenous to know the inside of my writer's mind." Often, thoughts came from Anthony's mouth, and he had little notion how puffed up they sounded.

He looked up, but not at me. He didn't see the dye on my head; he didn't see me at all.

I was as I ever was: his.

He studied the pages again, holding them up to the morning light. "She's an interesting artist, D." (He always called me D.) His delight in the matter had him pacing. Back and forth, his wheels turning. His grin was wide, as if slapped on his face. So often now, his facial expressions appeared to me so much like that of a child. He stood for a long time at the window looking out. He didn't share more with me. Then he gathered the parcel to his chest and went to the studio at the entrance of the villa and shut the door behind him.

After a while, I washed tomatoes from the garden in the sink. I heard him moving around, and then the pipes running. I went into the tiny bathroom and sat on the toilet while Anthony showered, and then I scanned the *Herald Tribune* that rested on the edge of the bidet.

"Do you want to sleep with her?" I asked him over the sound of the running water. How easy it was to be Anthony Borland, I thought. He laughed. "She's a fan, Daria, it's nothing." He opened the glass door of the shower to tell me more, such was his excitement. "Listen to this," he said, as if he were reading from one of the pages the young artist had sent. "You write from the point of view of a woman. Do you embody your characters' feminine spirit with lucid dreaming? Isn't that incredible, D? She really understands my writing."

You see, I knew it was already done. Anthony felt her presence in the village. He accepted the catcall she pitched up our quiet hill. I climbed in the shower with him and let go of the breath I'd been holding. He helped rinse the dark color from my hair until the water ran clear. Then he massaged the shampoo in and tended to the cream rinse and gently rinsed it again. He caressed my bottom as he got out of the shower. He was not an ungenerous man.

Not long after, the woman from the village arrived through the same wooden doors as her package; she demanded to know where his answers were. *My philosophical curiosities*, she called her questions, in her adorable English. Anthony smirked and took in her force. The girl was shiny, a fireball of intellect, confidence, and dark beauty, maybe a decade older than Louisa.

"You want my secrets? My artistic soul served on a platter?" Anthony teased her.

"Yes," she said, taking her time, considering it. "In a way," the woman said, "yes." She stopped to think when asked a question, as though in fact the whole world was waiting for her to respond. She pondered, like someone who'd endured the felt life of one thousand years.

Then this woman said more, not simply what Anthony might want to hear.

"I didn't care for this part." She pointed to a dog-eared page in his latest novel, from a worn copy she had carried in with her. She read his words aloud with scorn. She curled her lips when she spoke. She seemed to think that with her disapproval she could revise his printed words; she spoke with so much authority. Her eyes appeared as if they were gouged in black and she even stomped her feet; she was all show, all theatrics. Anthony laughed out loud, a towel around his shoulders, another around his waist.

I made coffee while Anthony excused himself to get dressed.

"Tell him to come to my atelier this afternoon," the woman said. "I want to show him my oils. Three o'clock," she said, and moved her hands up and down as if to say *more or less.* "You can

join in," she added. Our eyes didn't meet as she scrawled her
address on a piece of brown paper. She was in a hurry and gone
before the espresso pot made its rumble of power.

I remember thinking it then, when I told Anthony about
the invitation and watched his face fill with emotion. It was
inevitable they would sleep together.

I drank the coffee alone on the patio with the hard sun beating down on me.

He would not deny himself; this much I knew. So why stir
dust? Why rearrange the furniture over it, so to speak. My husband had nothing else in his head. Surely not his wife. But so
what? This woman was a rare opportunity on this finite planet.
After thirty years of marriage, jealousy has few fangs. We were
mature people now anyway. My husband was at times a brute,
but more often than not he was lost, like a wounded boy who
constantly needed guiding away from a hot stove or the check-
book.

Age deepens a person's wisdom.

It's like that joke: the call girl who comes to the door for a
man's eightieth birthday. "I'm here to give you super sex," she
tells the old man. "The way I feel," the old man says, "I'll just
take the soup."

We were not that ancient, of course. We were in our late
sixties but the rules still applied. Life continued to swirl, round
and round again. Thank God I had learned to observe.

Still, when Anthony went into town that afternoon, I followed him. Not out of despair or anger, I walked slowly, and
with purpose. The Ionian Sea town was deep in afternoon
slumber. Only the cats lingered about in the heat. Anthony was
a good forty paces ahead of me. Then I saw her, like a black line
on the empty street. I watched Anthony as he watched her. Her
long black dress took its time in a twisty saunter. Up the iron
staircase she went, in liquid motion.

Even from a distance her aura was powerful, a darkness that
had to do with antiquity and grace. My husband, the genius,
climbed the stairs after the woman.

I was no mouse. When I arrived at her address, I didn't hesitate. I went up. The terrace of her flat overlooked a lush vista of olive trees. The two of them were not stirred by my presence in the doorway. The young woman offered me a chair, but I refused. I stood and took in her spare apartment, making sure she was aware of the confident expression on my face.

It wasn't on my agenda to retrieve Anthony. I held my ground. I was calm.

She was explaining a large oil painting to him. It was a dramatic and well-executed scene of a couple in a boat. The female had gloomy curls and was paddling the oars with a red boa around her while the man reclined, smoking a cigarette; their faces were not visible. The artist spoke of Sappho, and her place in the history of the island seemed to seep from her pores. This was a woman who appeared to have little fear of death or poverty.

"This desk," she said, "is three hundred years old. This building—" she said and placed her hands against the Roman stone wall, "from the Byzantine era." My husband looked at the woman with something more than greed in his face. In turn, the woman seemed to want to devour the old writer. Hemingway's incarnation, some people called Anthony. How do I step inside you, was the big question the young woman had for my husband, as far as I could make out.

I had the thought: What surface would this ego romp of Anthony's undo now? Nothing, not even a tear in the fabric of me. I almost threw my hands up in the air. Then she came at me from the side. "What is your name?" she said up close to me.

"Daria." I said loudly, surprising myself.

"Daria, Daria, Daria." Over and over again, I said my name.

She laughed and walked around in a circle. I was a marionette, and she was pulling my strings. Anthony drank out of a jam jar, content, and wrote lines on a page. Lines to her, I presumed, while he sipped and wrote on A4 sheets, without looking at his wife. If he understood the tug of war between the two women in front of him, he pretended he did not.

The other woman's needs were clear. Anthony was the quest, and he was the one she would have. I watched my husband take a book from the shelf and listened as he read aloud to her. The man was so practiced at taking up space. Then I understood, like a shock it came to me watching his pandering, that this was the reward he had wanted all along. Idolatry.

Had I not provided it for him in three decades of love? Is that the moral of this story?

For instance, this diva had no name, or I do not recall one. She was only beautiful and headstrong, possibly a Taurus on the astrological chart. I imagined her in the local market, sassy to neighbors and fish sellers. No, desire and conquer was her raison d'être, what got her up in the mornings. I had no interest in interpreting the woman's shadows, ladling light back into her like the child she was. She was nothing to me.

In some way, though, in the moment, I longed to rescue my husband. I know. Pathetic. It was the same impulse I'd had when I'd nursed him from depression with my pea and ham soup, or when I took the train into Toronto to demand an advance from the publisher when his books were no longer a priority, and rent was due.

Anyway, it was clear that once this dance became human again, the crucible they'd spun would hit mortal ground. Selfish human habits and domestic routines would sear the seams off this thing. That was the one downfall of a person who desires: they are void of a future. Someone needs to do the washing up, for example.

Then the woman came close to me again, up to my face. "I think I want to be naked," she said casually. It was a challenge, a cold invitation for me to leave. I held her gaze. Anthony hooted. I am no mouse, I reminded myself. I unzipped my pencil skirt and pulled my stretched blouse over my head. I took everything off, slowly. I stood there in my lumpy, fleshy body. What was there to lose? I was in my truth. I went over to my husband and sat naked on his lap. I kissed him deeply.

I surprised even myself.

After that, there wasn't another move I could think of. I left them to it. I got up, put my clothes back on, descended the staircase, and went on my way.

The streets were filling up again with fruit vendors and the shop fronts rolled open once more. I walked slowly up the hill toward our lovely villa Tourterelle, and before going inside, I unpegged the laundry from the line, then snipped two fragrant pink roses from the hedge and set them atop the basket of clothes.

In the kitchen, Louisa was still in her robe. She was measuring the flour for tea biscuits at the tiny counter. "I'm making lemon biscuits, Ma," she said, "your favorite."

How nice.

"With late afternoon tea," I said to my daughter, and I went to her, took her face in my hands, and kissed her forehead.

"That will be something to look forward to."

You're Here Now

I knew Jimmy Pallotta was my birth father in the same way I knew the brown stain on my forearm was a birthmark. Everyone has a birthmark somewhere. Birthmark, birth father. They carried the same weight in my life. Besides, the man had eight other children; his plate runneth over.

I've never met Jimmy Pallotta but I'm on the way to his funeral. He died in a car crash two nights ago. A hit-and-run on Highway 5, according to the *Western Wheel*, our local paper. Alone this morning in my apartment I read the names of his children out loud from the obit page: Susan, Shaun, Anna, Danny, Connie, Patty, Kerry, Christina. The half-siblings I've never spoken to.

When I was younger, I'd spot them around our small Canadian town—in the Zehrs grocery and at the soccer field the one summer I played. Another time, in Donatella's Hair Salon, I sat in the chair behind Anna, who is nearest my age. Anna was having her long black hair cut into a French bob while I was having my pixie cut dyed platinum blond. She didn't notice me. I altered my look often back then. I had dreadful rainbows of colored hair and wore things like jean shorts with fishnets and Converse Hi-Tops. It was my practiced *I'm different* look, to show my individuality and my allegiance to my mother, Jean.

I was a single child to a single parent.

"It won't come up, Sylvie," Jean told me every time I fretted over how much I favored the Pallotta children, with my almond eyes and olive complexion. "You look just like me," she'd say. "Our faces match, and we're big boned." I believed my mother back then. Her words were my gospel. Every morning from the time I was eleven, I straightened my curls to look more like her perfect blond strands, which fell elegantly to her chin.

In the small prairie town where we lived, ethnic people stood out. Everyone knew the Chens, for example, because they were the only Asian family and they owned the 7-Eleven at Main and Pine. There were a handful of second-generation immigrant families in town; the Pallottas were the most prominent among them. They were "important" in ways my mother frowned upon. Jimmy Pallotta was famous for his quick and painless root canals. Rumor had it he'd give you a deal if you were down on your luck. Jean took me fifteen kilometers to High River, the next town over, for my dental checkups every six months.

Yes, my mother took care of everything. I didn't even know I resented her for it; it was just the air I breathed.

We were important in a different way—we had always traveled exotically, and I was an intellect's daughter. The pious worldly ones, we were, stuck in a one-horse town. At least that was the posture we liked to take.

Jean and I lived in a condo in the north end of Okotoks. The Pallotta family had a tract mansion in the south end, so my half-siblings and I went to different schools.

"They're a self-absorbed Latin family. They don't care for anyone outside their fold," my mother said, taking away any hope I had that they'd come looking for me. When their mother died of stomach cancer three years ago, I wrote a sympathy card to the family, thinking the affair with Jean might be less threatening since their mother was gone. I wrote the card a hundred times, but of course, I never sent it.

Now that I'm thirty-two years old, Jean and I talk less. I know my mother would prefer I were an eccentric academic living in Paris, but I'm quite the opposite. I'm a parole officer with long brown hair and I buy my clothes off the rack at Old Navy. I spend my days keeping tabs on murderers and drug cases and sending offenders back to jail if need be.

Anyway, the last time we spoke she brought up marriage again.

"They don't have any staying power, these men you date. All I want is a normal life for you."

"Felons do not inspire my dating pool, Mother."

"My feminist life wasn't the right thing after all. You need a shrink."

I've had a total of four boyfriends and ended it with each of them. I don't need to pay someone to tell me it's a pattern. A therapist would want to pillage through the effects of growing up fatherless. *No, thanks.*

In the crowded parking lot of Snodgrass Funeral Home, I find an empty spot near the entrance, as if it were reserved for me. It suddenly hits me, like a punch, that the man who has lived in my imagination for so long is gone forever. I won't ever meet him. Somewhere deep I must have had the childish idea that one day we'd spend hours in cafés talking or walking together along the Bow making up for lost time.

I have an urge to call my mother to tell her this, to tell her everything. But I deliberately tighten my hold on my purse where my cell is. When I wipe my boots on the entrance mat, I notice a tiny bud on a larch tree next to the heavy door. I inhale my deepest breath and join the crowd in the lobby.

Jimmy Pallotta's children are in a row at the entrance to the parlor, all tall, dark, and lean. They are lined up oldest to youngest. I wait my turn, barely breathing. Susan is first. "So sorry about your father," I say, almost boldly. "I'm Sylvie, Sylvie Young." My solar plexus tightens, and my ribs feel like steel pipes.

"Thank you," Susan says. It has to be hardest for the oldest. The woman looks a wreck.

"I'm sorry about your father." I say this to each of them. Their faces are familiar and beautiful. They are petite and are all black shine and heavy jewelry. *Dressed to the nines.* That's how my mother would describe them. She liked people who dressed to the nines. I have never been more aware of my big-bonedness and my plain style.

When I get to the end of the line, to Christina, the youngest, I suppress a gasp at how similar she appears to a sixth-grade photo of me, the one that I keep in my office drawer to remind myself not to let that little person down, that I am brave and should trust people and think good thoughts, not bad ones. I pause extra-long in front of Christina until the desire to hug her passes and I move on.

Once, in high school, when a boyfriend dragged me to the local Flyers hockey game, a man approached me. I recognized him as our town's crazy person, Johnny Rots. "You've got Danny Pallotta's face," he yelled, pointing at me. "That's Danny Pallotta's face." He said it three times. I put my face in my hands and my head between my knees. Danny, my half brother, could have been a few rows back for all I knew. The boyfriend laughed, like it was a joke. I darted out of the frozen building and later that night with a text I broke up with the boy.

Mother never regretted the affair with Dr. Pallotta, she says, because that would insult my existence. *He was the 'man seed' for your birth, full stop.* She obliterated any necessity for men in our world. It had always been just the two of us. La mère et la petite—a progressive duo. Our family was small and female: my mother, Grandmère, and my aunt Shirley. For twenty-nine years, until her retirement last fall, mother directed the Deerfoot Library Foundation and published heady articles about French-speaking Canada—it was our great national debate, the only debate: Would Quebec secede from the rest, even though it was smack in the middle of our country?

Once, when I was nine and we were waiting for a flight to Quebec City, I asked outright: "Maman, we're a weird family, right? Tu peux me dire." I had tears in my eyes and my mother, never one to bend the truth for a child's sake, said, "Bien sur, Sylvie. Don't be daft?" The story became part of our family lore.

"Why don't we bolt from barren Alberta and move to Montreal?" I often asked her.

"Grandmère won't live forever, and we live like queens here on my single salary."

It used to be an event, visiting Grandmère at Dorchester Manor every Tuesday night and the three of us sharing a 'happy hour' meal in her room. Now I arrive alone in time to watch *Jeopardy* with her and leave right after. Aunt Shirley used to come to us for supper on Fridays too, and Mother and my aunt would cackle over stories from their youth. Mother would brighten with her older, funnier sister and I'd try to hide my obvious jealousy over what I'd never have: a sibling. But Aunt Shirley hasn't come in months and mother seems content most nights to eat curry take-away and watch old movies on TCM.

Now, kneeling in front of the dead person from whom I've inherited my Roman nose, I can't imagine what it might have been like to have a father. This man, who looks kindly and handsome, even in death. The creases in his face must have endeared his children to him.

Occasionally, I envisioned myself with the siblings all crammed on the sectional with bowls of gnocchi in our laps, watching *60 Minutes*; other times I'd see us all hanging from trees, singing like the Von Trapps. But mostly I suppressed these fantasies. It would have been a disastrous contrast—eight rowdy siblings for part of the week and the rest of the time in our monosyllabic condo, mother working under a lone bulb at the kitchen table.

But the thing is, I don't want to leave the funeral home. I take a seat in a back pew and watch each of the siblings. Anna and Connie hold each other beside a screen of lily wreaths and Shaun and Susan nod to a group of prominent townies, including the mayor and a corrupt lawyer, whom Mother can't stand. Suddenly, an ache of regret rushes through me, almost violent, like rage, because my mother never let me near these people. *The family*. She never let me decide for myself.

"What did you say your name was?" It's Danny, the youngest Pallotta son, he sits beside me on the pew. Danny is the one Johnny Rots said had my face. *Jesus*.

"Sylvie," I say without looking at him.

"Thanks for coming, eh." I can feel his stare but can't make myself look at him. Danny is two years younger than me and has a police record: B&E and petty crime. I keep a daily watch on his file at work.

"He was a well-respected man," I say.

"Best root canal in town. That's how he afforded the eight of us."

Nine, I want to say. But the root canal expert didn't afford *me.* When my mother told Jimmy she was pregnant he said he'd give her a thousand bucks, five hundred for an abortion and five hundred to keep her mouth shut. She took the first five hundred and considered an abortion, but she wasn't a woman you kept quiet.

"A real tragedy," I say, and all at once I feel as if I might cry. I can't believe I'm sitting beside my half brother and I'm hearing his voice and we're having a conversation and I know so much about him.

"I thought it'd be suicide."

"Excuse me?"

"He was a lone wolf. Dentists have the highest suicide rate."

"I didn't know."

Then he bends his head low and makes a steeple with his fingers.

"Listen, I know why you're here," he says.

I hold my breath and don't move a muscle.

"Me and my sisters, we knew about you."

I can't speak. Even as a wave of relief takes hold. I let out an audible sigh.

"My dad was no saint, eh? My sisters are clannish but I feel bad for ya."

I look around to see if the others have their eyes on me. Any moment the pack of them might surround me. And yet, the feeling is there, that this is my due. In a way, I long for the wrath of this big family. Whatever punishment is coming to me for being alive, I'm ready for it.

"It's like I'm looking in a mirror." He laughs, and he sounds just like Frank, one of my parolees.

"I better go." But a part of me wants to say, *Yes, I am your sister. Now what do we do?*

"I'm just telling you if you ever need anything."

"What would I need?"

"You showed. You must want something."

"Honestly, I'm not sure why I came."

"He was a shit father, if that's any consolation. We kind of raised ourselves. Like a bunch of guinea pigs rolling in mud till we found the nipple."

"Guinea pigs?" I imagine he's thinking of the ways his father failed him in order to mask his own failings with the cheap crime ring he's got himself into.

"Do you want to meet everyone?" He gestures toward the crowd.

"Oh, god. No."

"You're here now."

"I'm leaving."

"Even the little ones know."

"I shouldn't have come."

"It says something about you. Coming on the day of his funeral."

"You don't know anything about me."

"I know you're my sister."

I drive back to my apartment through the late winter slush and the feeling of the days getting longer. It's 3:30 and I should be at the corrections office meeting with Joe, one of my parolees. Joe held up Chen's 7-Eleven last year and he's fresh out on bail. I need to collect myself with tea at the kitchen table. *A cup of tea solves the world's problems.* That's my mother's voice in my head. It never stops telling me the right way to do things. As I sit by the window with my tea, the sun beams warmth onto my side. I think of Jean and the fact that she reads *The Wheel* every morning, paying particular attention to the births and deaths, and yet she hasn't called.

There's a knock at the door and it's like a shock running

through me. No one visits my apartment. Without making a sound I move toward the door and look through the peephole. It's Anna Pallotta, the one closest to my age, with young Christina. Anna's holding the girl's hand and the girl is crying. I lean my back against the door without breathing. The bell rings again.

"Yes?" I say, opening the door slowly.

They are still in their fancy black dresses and heavy jewelry. Against my dreary hallway the scene seems far from reality.

"You've upset my little sister. Way to go." Anna is wobbly in high heels and the girl has red lipstick on. Anna leans oddly against the door, and her gaze is unfocused. Is she drunk?

"I'm sorry," I say.

"Daddy's body is barely cold."

"I'm truly sorry."

"Did you come to collect? Is that it?"

"What? I think you should leave now."

"Now you want a piece of the pie, right?"

I've always wondered about Anna. I've seen her working the checkout at Zehrs and yet a few years back she was in the *Wheel*, which announced her law degree from University of Calgary. Something must have happened, something pretty major for her to come back to work a minimum-wage job in town. These people are a puzzle, so different from me, and Danny with his record, and their philandering father.

"I don't want anything. I was paying my respects."

"Stay away from us." The look from Anna is pure hatred. She stumbles a bit and grabs her sister by the hand.

"You're a slut," Christina blurts out, and then they turn their backs and walk back toward the elevator.

"It's not my fault," I say.

I don't know what I'm saying. Anna laughs and runs her hand along the wall in swirls. They don't turn back. The elevator door closes and I stand there.

"None of it had anything to do with me," I say to the empty hallway.

Days pass. I come and go from work like a criminal and I haven't talked to Jean. One afternoon, when I return from lunch at the courthouse cafeteria there's a note under my office door.

Dear Sylvie,

We'd like to get to know you. Please come to Shaun's house for lunch on Sunday. 3 p.m.

225 Woodgate Drive.

The Pallotta family

இ

On Saturday, the day before the Sunday lunch invitation, I ride my bike along the sidewalk for the one kilometer it takes to get to my mother's condo. The note from the Pallotta siblings is zipped inside my blue windbreaker. I'm strangely propped up from the invitation.

It's noon and there are tiny puddles on the road and little snowdrops and crocuses popping white and yellow on the green parkway. A robin's trill breaks the silence, a sure sign of spring's arrival and good things to come. At my mother's door, there are two bright pots of daisies, and suddenly I'm irritable.

"Hello, petal," mother says, giving me an airy kiss. She's right out of an advert for geriatric meds, with her gardening gloves and pruning shears, CBC Radio 1 blaring from the kitchen. "Have you eaten?"

"Why didn't you tell me?" I flip off my sneakers.

"About?" She walks toward the atrium and continues tending to her orchids, her obsession since retirement.

"My father's dead."

"He was not your father."

"I went to the funeral, Ma, and you know what? They've known about me all along." I feel the blood gathering in my cheeks. I'm laughing when I want to scream. Why haven't I questioned her more? I've been her puppet all along.

"Oh, brother." She sits, puts the shears and gloves on the sofa cushion, and folds her hands in her lap. She has tears in her eyes, but to me it looks like defiance.

"I'm their sister and they've invited me to lunch tomorrow."
I can't believe I'm telling it all at once. "Goddammit, Mother.
You had a sister, right? You got to have a sister."

"You don't need this now. You have a busy life, darling."

"I'm thirty-two and I have no fucking life."

"Would you like a cup of tea? I'm brewing Earl Grey."

"I've got my job and you and Grandmère, but what else? I
want another chance."

"Petal, they'd never accept you as their own. You'd be opening a can of worms."

"You're the authority on everything, eh?"

"Nothing good can come of it."

"You can't control me anymore."

"Darling, whatever you're looking for, it isn't them. It's
something you need to find in yourself. You're searching again."

"What if something great can come of it, Mother?"

"Spring makes you nostalgic. You know this. April is the
cruelest month."

"Don't you understand? I might be able to have a relationship with his children. My sisters and brothers."

She walks into the kitchen and clicks off the loud radio.

"I can't be you, Mother. Have a child alone, then soldier on
and dive into work and make the best of it. That's not who I
am."

"Find a boyfriend then. That might solve it all."

"I'm leaving, Mother. You've morphed into some retrograde
granny."

"You're bullying me now. It's the wrong thing to do, Sylvie."

She follows me through the rooms of my childhood. I push
my feet into my shoes and grab my bike helmet, knocking a
potted orchid to wobbling.

"Listen to your mother, Syl."

"Where is your fire anymore? You've become so fearful, the
kind of person you used to despise."

"Get out of my house then," she says. "You need to sort out
your priorities and you owe me an apology."

I leave quickly through the front door and make my way on my bike the same way I came, through the empty, flat streets with dull reflections in the puddles. I pass my turn and ride miles out along the flat prairie road toward the township of Blackie, and when I'm completely exhausted, I turn around. Back at my apartment I shower and climb into bed. It's only seven in the evening but I'm gone, asleep.

The next morning, I eat granola from the box and drink tea. I drive to my favorite bench, my brooding bench from long ago, overlooking the Bow River and opaque Big Rock, the place I used to run away to when I was a little girl. I stay for hours just thinking and watching the river. At two o'clock, I get back in the car and drive out to the new subdivision with the golf course, and park in front of 225 Woodgate Drive. It's a giant European brick home with an iron gate and a gaudy cement fountain in front.

In the driveway, a young boy is taking shots on a girl who's playing goalie in net. It's Christina, the one who called me a slut. My youngest half sister. I swallow and my body is aflutter with nerves. I get out of the car and the two of them run toward me and I step back, then lean against the hood of my car.

"I'm Christina," the girl says, smiling, offering a hand. "Peace?"

I take her hand but I don't say a word. From my parolees I know such changes of heart are rarely legit.

"This is my nephew, Frankie," the girl says. "They're all inside waiting for you."

"Thanks," I say, comparing this girl to the sting of the scene she made at my apartment with her older sister. Every inch of me wants to turn. *Run,* my mind says. I could be at home with tea by the window and later eat stir-fry watching *Friends* reruns. My heart is pumping fast. The door opens and Danny is there.

"Hey everyone, it's Sylvie," Danny announces back into the house. His smile is kind and I feel a slight release in my jaw.

"I was betting on you," he says and shakes my hand, and then pats my shoulder and guides me in.

"And the others?"

"About fifty-fifty that you'd show." He laughs. "Can I take your coat?"

"I'm fine."

"Welcome." It's Anna, the drunk one. *Oh, Jesus.* "You must have thought I was insane. I apologize for coming to your place." She comes toward me, laughing, her hands out. She is plain, less scary. She's wearing plaid pajama bottoms and a Calgary Flames jersey.

"Did my little sister apologize too?"

"She was fine."

"Truth is, I got kind of messed up about my dad and went a little loco. So, yeah, it was my idea to have you here. All out in the open like." Anna is thin—almost sinewy—something I did not inherit in the gene pool.

Against my better judgment, I want to believe that she has good intentions. Something about her casual openness puts me at ease. "I've seen you a few times at Zehrs," I tell her.

"I'm the only grocery girl with a law degree. I'm a nanny for my sibs now too." She pauses. "Props to you for showing up here."

"It's a little daunting, for sure." I have been so blind; I see now it's fear that fuels me. Like mother, like daughter.

"We act rough-and-tumble. Christ, I was in rehab after college. I went all the way down. But I've seen the light."

She takes me through the kitchen; she's uncomfortably close to me. "Please eat. We are an army of mouths to feed but this is ridiculous." There are loaves of Italian bread piled on the counter, stacks of pizza boxes, cookies and cakes in tiers of packaging, and a tray of cold cut subs. It's more food than I've ever seen.

"Here's my advice," Susan tells me, taking over for Anna when we are in the family room. "Take a seat next to the fireplace. Let us come to you." There's more food on a card table, in aluminum trays: a lasagna and two vats of pastas, roasted potatoes, bowls with salads, and cases of beer and pop. I sit in the oversized burgundy chair, as instructed, glad my back is to the wall. Danny hands me a glass of red wine.

"My father's chianti," he says.

"Thank you." I know I won't drink it. It's three in the afternoon.

The siblings are assembling, all talking and laughing, and I try to ward off my worry that they despise me and are looking for ways that I am less than them. Even the way they arrange themselves in a semicircle seems to show that I am outside of what has always been theirs.

"Sylvie, welcome to our home. I'm Shaun and this is my wife, Linda."

"Hello." I look from one to the other. They are all such pretty people.

"Did you meet Frankie out front?"

I tell them yes and hear myself say mundanities about their lovely home and their cute son. Frankie, I realize, is my nephew. Anna does the rest of the introductions, all of them staring at me as their names are called. I feel lightheaded. Luckily, Anna is swift with it. Her movements are so rapid she must be on some kind of speed. It occurs to me that I'm in my brother's house without anything to offer and nothing to say. It goes against Jean's cardinal rule of always bringing the host a gift, a flower, a handwritten note.

Susan hands me a plate of penne with meatballs.

Patty is sitting cat-like on the carpet. She is twisting her dark curls and staring off, not in protest, just not present. She has a wildness in her eyes, and I can't stop looking her way. Kerry and Connie are outstretched on a recliner opposite me. They have that entitled teenager way about them, as if they have life by the tail. Susan is the most normal. She's sitting upright, looking attentive, as if she understands how it might feel to meet eight strangers who are my next of kin. She gives dirty looks to her younger sisters. God, there must be a million dynamics between them all.

If things had gone differently, they would have been in my

life every day, and I'd have complicated relationships with each of them. I can handle the most hardened thugs one-on-one, but this is beyond me.

"God, you look so much like Dad," Susan says, and Anna starts to cry.

I want to say sorry but mother has drilled that out of me. *Why are Canadians always begging forgiveness?* I sideways smile and say nothing.

"Susan, don't be such a *stronza*," Danny says. "She can't help it, can she?"

"Wish I looked like him," Susan says, and I want to cover my face like I did at the arena so many years ago. We are all quiet for a moment, and then it's like a tidal wave: they ask about my work and the criminals, they fire names at me to see if we know the same people in town. They want to know who I'm dating. They want the list of every friend I've ever had, it seems. They debate the merits of penne versus rigatoni.

Susan sits on the arm of my chair. "For years it was our mother," she says, leaning in. "We were so protective of her. But now we're orphans and everything has changed. Come for lunch every Sunday to start. Then we'll bring you in for the birthdays and weddings and every little thing we celebrate. It's time."

The doorbell rings, and I get up. It's an older Italian couple at the entrance with carnations in a vase and a tray covered in foil. I take the opportunity to move toward the door while the others are shifting. I slip into my shoes and put my windbreaker over my shoulder. Behind the couple is someone else. My god. It's my mother.

"What are you doing here?" I murmur, exasperated. I feel embarrassed and ashamed.

"Thought I'd join you."

I'm in shock. "Are you crazy?"

"I want to meet everyone too."

"Mother! They didn't invite you." I want her gone.

"We're a package deal," she says, still approaching. "Isn't that our motto?"

"This is different. I'm blood with these people."

"Don't leave yet, Sylvie." Anna is there beside me and takes notice of my mother. It's as if Anna is my ally now. My sister is asking me to stay.

"Go home, Jean," I tell my mother. "I'm going back inside. I'll see you later, okay?"

My mother has no choice. She looks sad and small as she walks away from the porch. I go inside with Anna; I stay for another half hour. It doesn't feel right. They are talking among themselves and trying to include me when they can. But what they say, their references, seem to come from a different galaxy.

I know I'll carry the image of my mother walking away from that house all the years of my life. Back in my car, the tears come. *Nothing good can come of it, nothing good can come of it...* echoes in my mind, my mother's warning. I think of their faces and what each of them held when they looked at me. Each of them with their difficulties and resentments and grief.

Out of nowhere, *Lo! He Comes with Clouds Descending*, Grandmère's Anglican hymn, fills my mind. It tumbles off my lips like a prayer I didn't ask for. I drive to Dorchester Manor and park my Honda. I don't get out: it's enough that Grandmère is in there and safe. I let the tears fall onto the steering wheel.

Later I retreat to my lonely bench under the arms of the nesting willow tree at Big Rock. I've been hiding there since I was a girl, always with the hope that Jean would come and find me. She always did. And now the truth comes at me: those people aren't really mine for the taking. They never were.

And if mother is looking for me, this is where I'll be.

FORT PIERCE, FLORIDA

In 1948 she moved to Ft Pierce, Florida, where she wrote a series of magazine and newspaper articles while working as a maid and a substitute teacher.

—*The Baltimore Sun*

Mouths don't empty themselves unless the ears are sympathetic and knowing.

—Zora Neale Hurston, *Mules and Men*

Here is a white man, outside the open door of this motel room. He's slightly yellow around the eyes, the bones in his face pushing out. He's a balding, youngish person, with thin, pale hands, in a slept-in white shirt. "I don't think I want maid service now," he mutters at her. But then he smiles.

"Well," she tells him, "you got it anyway."

"You're new."

"Been here a while."

"Never seen you."

She shrugs. "I've been here."

After she enters, it takes her a second to gather herself. It's been three days now. The slightest motion and she's out of breath. It's almost as if she must come back to her body from her pain. She has six rooms to clean on this floor alone.

She pulls the bedspread off the bed, ignoring the typewriter and the pages under the lamp by the telephone. He waits there by the doorway, watching.

"Do you want me to leave, sir?" she asks him.

"What's your name?"

In this part of the country, they can ask you anything. They can be openly curious about you and demand to know your name. And you'd better answer.

"Zora," she tells him.

"Funny name."

"What's yours?"

He looks at her. It's clear he isn't accustomed to being spoken to like this by a domestic. "Okay. My name's Bodie. That satisfy you?"

"Last or first?"

"Bodie Smith."

"Funny name," she says softly.

He smiles. "Yeah. Sure it is." He comes a little way into the room and sways slightly, stopping to wipe his mouth with the back of one hand. Then he rocks on his feet and looks her way, his hands going into his pockets, *Like an idler*, she thinks.

"Where're you from, Zora?"

"Not far from here, but I been around," she says, raising her weary face to his smile, noticing the empty bottles near the typewriter.

She pauses but doesn't say more.

He walks to the table and looks down at the typewriter. "You always frown like that?"

"I got a headache," she says. "Had it three days."

"That's awful."

"It is that."

"Yeah," he says. "Do you feel you have to comment on everything I say?"

"Sure don't," she says, then adds, "Sir."

He smiles again. "So you're from Florida. Where've you been—around?"

"Last trip was to the West Indies."

"You serious?"

She nods, but he doesn't see this.

"You're serious."

"I was studying the people there, yes, sir."

"Where exactly?"

Is he from the newspapers? The ones that published lies about her in the North? "British Honduras," she says.

"Ever met a writer before?"

Does he recognize her? She looks into his glassy eyes. Maybe he's just talking. She glances at the pages and the typewriter. She reads the first line of the writing:

Milton Grayfield's mouth opened to take in the cigarette like a bat flying into a cave.

Bad, bad, bad.

She looks at him and feels sorry, knowing how hard writing is. But she doesn't much like him. What he's thinking of her is simple and the same as ever, and everywhere she goes all the time people think the same thing. She blows air from her lips.

"So, you a writer?"

His eyes narrow. "You a writer, *sir*." She walks toward the door.

He smiles slowly, tottering a little and then straightening himself. "Yeah, I guess we can ignore the custom of the country for now, can't we." It is not a question.

"Well?" she says. "Are you?"

"I take it that you know how to read and write," he says.

"I can do that."

"Where'd you learn?"

"I went to college…" She pauses and puts both thumbs to her temples where the pain is. "Sir."

Now he grins and actually makes a small chuckling sound. "Score one for the colored lady."

She is at the door now.

"You through?" he asks.

"No, but you said you didn't want it. And I've got twelve other rooms to do today."

"Well, maybe I do want it."

"If you could make up your mind, sir, that would be good."

"Stay as long as it would take to clean the room but talk to me instead."

She holds on to the door frame and watches him turn the armchair and sit in it, so he can see her. "You want to talk, sir," she says. "All right." She leans on the frame, folding her arms.

"I'm writing about a young guy, a tragic, depressed, romantic, usually drunk guy, living in the South and trying to write a novel."

She manages to keep a straight face.

"I thought I was almost finished until today. I'm renting this room by the week. I've been here six months. My family's against it. My father especially. You know Bodie Molasses Company? That's my father."

"I always liked molasses," she says.

"I always wanted to write, you know?"

"Well, you got to do what you love." The pressure of her headache keeps her from moving.

"I'm going places." He pulls a flask out of his back pocket, opens the lid and drinks, then holds it out to her.

"No, sir. Too early in the day for me."

"Sun's up. It's past five somewhere, as they say."

"You won't go far with that stuff, sir," she tells him.

"Demons in the bottle?"

"Something like that."

He takes another drink. "I can go into the depths of truth with this stuff."

"That so?"

"You've got a nice, soft voice. I'd call it cool. It's peaceful. And, yes, I think so about this here bourbon." He holds up the flask again.

"You can go into the depths of losing your car. You can learn all there is to learn about going to the bathroom in the street, or sleeping there, for that matter."

"You sound like my mammy now."

She shifts, shaking her head at him, but he isn't looking at her. She thinks he might be drunk. "I'm going to leave you now," she says.

"Hey, what did you study in college?" he asks.

"Anthropology. Literature."

"And you're an expert, then, on these things."

"I've studied them," she says. "Sir."

He gets up and crosses to the table and sits there, one hand on the pages, as if to keep them from being blown by some invisible wind. "Then what're you doing here?"

"Research."

He drinks from the flask, has some trouble closing it, and then sets it down on the desk. "Research," he says. "You're kidding me, right? Researching what?"

"The life of a domestic."

"You needed to experience that."

"I do, yes."

He's such a boy and he doesn't know a damn thing. Part of her wants to show him, tell him a bit about life, what it is to be a writer first, a Black writer second, and a Black female writer in the South, but she doesn't care about this kid and none of it means anything in the moment. She's a maid. Back here, in Nowhere, Florida. Alone. Out of print. And still going about her days, still heading for the horizon, at least in her mind—that burns. It does burn. It's as if every thought rakes the inside of her skull.

The young man sits forward. "You're probably an expert on good English."

She nods, but only slightly, just enough to indicate that she's heard him. She can't believe she's still wasting her time here. But she has not given up one iota of her dignity. She'll sell him a library's worth of books if that's what he wants. She straightens and holds on to the faith that she'll always get by.

"I didn't finish school," he says. "What school'd you go to? Was it up north?"

"Well, yes."

"Do I have to pry every word from you? Where'd you go? We're friends now."

"Howard University in Washington, DC."

"Never heard of it."

"That says something about you."

"Really. Aren't *you* proud."

"I'm being truthful."

"Aren't you being a bit uppity too?"

There's a moment of silence. He's waiting, with that half-smile on his face.

"Not for me to say, is it, sir?"

"Uppity, all right," he says. But he's smiling. "I don't mind."

"If that's how you see it."

"And you can stop the *sir* shit."

She waits.

"Sorry about the language," he says. "Ma'am." A moment later he says, "Howard University."

She sighs from the pounding pain in her head and knows he thinks it's because of the conversation. "Not a bad institution," she tells him. "But I've taken education wherever and however I could find it."

He seems to be thinking about this. "And you're working here as a maid."

"Everything has something to teach us," she says.

"You're not like most of the colored ladies. You talk like you know me."

"Maybe I do," she says.

"It's true. Not like any of the colored ladies around here."

"And how many do you know?"

"A few," he says.

"I'm not sure I believe it."

"There's no reason for me to lie about it. I don't have any trouble with you. I think it's terrible what has been done to you people."

"Poor ol' us, huh?" She laughs and then winces. He's just a boy at the beginning, a boy with a rich daddy. She thinks of that molasses and how much money his father must have. "When I was a little child," she says, "I used to climb a tree in front of the house where I lived, and I'd look out at the horizon. That was the most interesting thing to me, all the way back then. I knew I wanted to see what the end of the world was like."

"You must've had a terrible life."

"My daddy was mayor of the town where I lived. Quite a

life. But then my mother died and I had to spend time in different houses—relatives."

"I did that too. My folks have been getting divorced off and on for twenty years."

She was hoping to work this evening on her novel about the Jews, and Herod—a big project for which she has high expectations. She glances again at the stack of pages on the desk in front of the young man.

He's looking at them too. He lifts one corner of the manuscript and lets it fall. "I'm stuck," he says. "I don't know what the next line is."

"Say anything," she says without thinking about it. "It'll probably lead to something else."

"You sound like you know about it."

"Matter of fact, I do."

"A highly educated colored lady."

She says nothing.

"Never met a ni—a *negro* with a degree, now that I think of it."

A moment later he opens the drawer of the desk and brings out a little half-pint bottle. She watches him open it and take a swallow. "You ever write a book?"

Now she can tell him—but finally there isn't any reason to. She doesn't need the books to hold up to anybody, to prove her worth. She shakes her head. "It's crossed my mind."

"Maybe you should."

"Maybe I will."

"You got a husband?"

"I did."

"He die?"

"No."

"And you're doing research."

"For myself, yes."

"You figured anything out?" He takes a long swallow from the little bottle.

"Some things," she says. "I'm patient."

He's staring at the pages on the desk. "Don't have any idea what's next. It's killing me."

"You got a girl?"

This seems to shake through him. "Sure. She's not speaking to me though. Doesn't think I'm much, you know?" He pauses and looks up at her. "I've got a feeling you don't think I'm much either," he says.

"I learned a long time ago not to make quick judgments about people, sir."

"How old are you?"

"Oh, old as the hills."

"Yeah. You want to hear the beginning of my novel?"

"No."

He looks at her and begins to laugh, shaking his head. "Yeah. Well."

In her closet of a room off the highway, not three miles from here, are all her books, published and unpublished. And many letters, notes, journals—her passions, obsessions, and her arguments, the profound friendships and laughs, the fights and the struggles—and she has wondered if it is all ending now, the way it seems to be, with this one long headache.

She has left her world to come back to this hovel of a town again; she hasn't told anyone where she is or what she's doing. They've tried, so many of them, to bring her down. They lied about her and spread terrible rumors, and she had to prove that she was out of the country as an alibi for a charge that still appalls her, still makes her lose her train of thought. To think that anyone would believe that she could do what they accused her of—seducing a ten-year-old boy. There has been a low-grade nausea in her ever since. She looks at the young man now, in his increasing drunkenness, shuffling the pages of his supposed novel.

He rubs his eyes and then regards her. "You look like you're about to fall over," he says. "Are you all right?"

"I'm all right."

"You're holding awful tight to that door frame."

She stands upright and feels her legs grow heavy. So much of what she has written turns out to be true in the viscera and nerves. She thinks of the lines in her book *Dust Tracks on the Road* about faithfulness and being steadfast. Keep on, she tells herself.

"You won't look at the first page of this?" he says, standing.

"I've got my own work to do, sir." The migraine is worse than any she's ever felt. She reaches for the door again.

"I know," he says. "Twelve rooms."

She stands straighter and turns, then sits on the foot of the bed, surprising herself. One of her stockings has dropped to her ankle, and she feels suddenly too old to move. But she runs her hands across the lap of her uniform skirt and regards him. He's looking at an old Black woman who seems a motherly servant to him. "Just the first couple of sentences," she says.

He picks up a page and reads the sentence about the cigarette and the bat in the cave and looks at her. She sees the same hunger for life in his eyes, the same wild hope to find the other side of the horizon.

She starts to lie, hating that she has to. "Why, that's really quite—" But now she stops. She will not actually lie. "Quite interesting."

"You think so?"

"I would say so, yes, sir."

"Can I read on?"

"If you have to," she says.

He goes on. The smoking of the cigarette occupies the first three pages. It is described in minute detail, and she loses the thread of it. There's no tension—only the rich guy and the cigarette and the smoking.

He stops. "What do you think?"

"I'm impressed by it," she manages. It occurs to her that there's no way to help him. Even if it *were* good.

"It seems dead," he sighs.

"They all do until the life gets breathed into them," she says. "Keep going."

He stares. "Who *are* you?"

"Pardon?"

"You're a teacher. Why're you doing this stuff with the cleaning."

"I told you."

"Will you listen to more of it?"

She puts her hands to her head. "I'm in pain."

"It's that bad, and you're being nice to me."

"Are you talking about my headache or the fact that I'm still here?"

"I was talking about the writing."

"Go ahead and read another page."

He looks at the pages in his hands and then hands them over to her.

She takes them and waits for him to speak.

"The grammar's all wrong, isn't it?"

The grammar looks fine. She reads a half page about sipping a glass of bourbon. She hands the page back to him.

"Well?" he says. "Tell me the truth."

"I have done that in every instance of my life." She has the thought that perhaps he might be teachable. "It's vivid," she tells him. "But it's not doing anything yet."

He waits.

"Start it sooner," she says.

"Start what? Make him younger?"

"No—start the drama. Make trouble for him."

He looks down at the pages, then he walks to the table, where he puts them down. Drinking from the bottle again, he turns to her. "I haven't made any trouble for him?"

"Not in those pages," she says. "Not in what I saw."

"He's severely depressed."

"You have to indicate that."

"Who *are* you?"

"I'm the woman who came to clean your room."

"But you're a teacher. You've taught school."

"Yes—and I've worked for newspapers too."

"So you *are* a writer."

She thinks of the project on her table at home, and all the silences of the past few years, trying to get toward what she's striving to accomplish—and so many bad reactions to the last novel, about the white woman, poor Arvay Henson, striving for identity, for some kind of true expression of herself. Why indeed can't a colored woman tell the story of a white woman, and make it true? People have no trouble believing the worst things about others; why not search for something good and true and possible in the life under the skin?

"You are," the young man says, "aren't you."

She says, "The important thing to decide is if *you* are."

"Tell me how to do it," he says.

"Just say the truth," she tells him. "Find out what it is and tell it."

He sits down and puts his hands up to his face. "I'm drunk."

"I've got to finish," she says, heading for the door.

"Thank you," he says, so quietly that she almost misses it.

As she closes the door on him, she thinks, maybe he'll learn to do it somehow, maybe he won't.

From this balcony she can see the shoreline. Big, dark birds are circling out over the water. They aren't gulls. She watches them. Vultures? Pelicans? But they're circling. Pelicans don't circle—they sail low, just above the water. Well, but now the birds swoop and do just that.

Pelicans, then.

Her headache seems to be easing, out in the open air. She's afraid to trust it. She has to take care of these rooms and collect her pay, then get to the store. The refrigerator's empty. There's nothing to eat in the house. The money is so bad that she can't pay her bills, and the pressure is beating her. In the little paper-cluttered house, there's her work—what matters most. The only thing that matters. The pages wait for her, on the small table inside the door. Her work: her unruly, willful, tolerant companion, her constant.

TEACUPS

When Claire and I and her youngest, baby Nedi, arrive at Lettieri Café in Yorkville, the singletons of our little therapy group—Yves and Elena—are already there. Only Claire and I are married; she has a big family and I haven't had mine yet. That's why I need therapy in the first place. There has been tension in our house; I'll say it: trouble. It's gotten to where Toby and I barely speak to each other. *Oh, you've already eaten? Here's the mail. Your mother called.* It's like that mostly. He makes rules I'm supposed to be happy with—he says "no" to a marriage counselor and a dog, but "yes" to infrequent upside-down sex.

Nedi, who is fourteen months, had fallen asleep in the back of my minivan, and I managed to get her into the new stroller I ordered online, without her waking or crying. Claire lets out a sigh as she sits down next to Yves in the booth, knowing she can relax while I'm around. Yves gently slides a steaming pot of mint tea and an empty glass mug in front of Claire. For me, he's ordered an americano with an extra shot of espresso, the way I like it. He's the mother hen of our group.

We are three women and one gay man. We began in a formal group-therapy setting—clinical, you might say. After a particularly stalemated session with our therapist, Julia, we stumbled together toward the subway, and Yves, who was going through hell with his wife after owning up to his longtime lover, Daniel, said, "Let's save the cash and meet up for coffee instead." Yves is a businessman who made a fortune in a start-up. *If you ladies are in, meet me at Lettieri at ten o'clock, Wednesday mornings.*

Each of us had our way of letting Julia down. She's a good therapist, but there was something about being in the front room of her fourteenth-floor apartment, we later admitted, that made us feel like actors, going around the room confessing our weaknesses and sorrows, while she sat there magisterially with her perfectly groomed black hair tucked ever so slightly under her chin. I could have imagined this, but her chair seemed higher than ours. The director with all her pretty material things and then us, the troubled ones.

After a session one night, Julia led us to her fancy dining room, and on her oak farm table were stacked various patterned china cups, plates, and bowls. She didn't want them anymore, she said, and offered them to us. As I stuffed a flowery teacup with a mismatched saucer into my Roots backpack, I thought, *She doesn't even think we can set a proper table.* That's what finally did it for me.

The other members of the group stayed on with Julia, and it's just as well. With the four of us, we don't have to talk about our childhood traumas or feel pressed to make stuff up if there isn't any bullshit from the week. Julia fancied a juicy anecdote, some slippage, and in a way we all wanted to please her, wanted her to take pity on us, so she'd keep us under her wing. It wasn't healthy. At the coffee shop, we gloss over our pain if we feel like it. "We are those mismatched teacups," I told everyone last week, surprising myself with my tone of comradery and schmaltz.

Today, as usual, Claire begins, because she needs it more than the rest of us. She speaks quickly, laughing as she talks. She's like a pressure cooker letting out some of the steam of her disastrous life in puffs of humor.

"So, we're at this family gathering," she tells us, "his aunt's back lawn, and a few of his Pakistani friends are there. There are so many fucking mosquitoes, you know? And this photographer guy is taking pictures of my girls and they're clowning around. Anyway, I got out my can of Off and handed it to one of the mothers whose teenage boys were scratching their legs so hard it looked like white chalk etched on their ankles.

"The mother said 'no' to me, and the boys pleaded with her, you know, like, 'Please. We're being eaten alive.' So I give them the Off. 'You've suffered long enough,' I say.

"But the mother gives it back to me again. 'No,' she tells

me, like I've tried to give them cocaine or something. My husband gives me this look, and then I know. I've crossed some line. I'm always crossing some fucking line. So, in the car, I tell him to take me to my mother's even before he has a chance to say it, but he says it anyway. 'You were flirting with those boys.' Imagine it. 'You were flirting with them!' he tells me. Fifteen and thirteen years old, these kids. Fifteen and thirteen. *You were flirting with them.*" She imitates her husband's stern, accented voice so well it makes us laugh. "So, we're living at my mother's again."

We three others steal glances at each other while she talks. No one else understands how she got to this place. Her husband, stuck in a misogynist century, the eleventh century for God's sake, and Claire, sprightly and intelligent and lovely, could have had her pick of men. But I get it. She has her three baby girls. No matter what. Once, Claire told us about the guys she had dated before Mustafa—noncommittal types, guys in bands, bartenders, etc. Mustafa told her he loved her on the first date and he wanted a family with her.

Even with this horrendous story she's just told I contemplate the security of a guy who knows what he wants and thinks of himself as a provider. Even if that is something I shouldn't be thinking of as a staunch feminist, I entertain it. Toby once said that he didn't want to have kids until he had five million dollars in the bank.

"My advice to you two," Claire says to Yves and Elena. "Marry someone who looks like you."

Elena glances down at her phone, unaware of what is being implied. She is the young one, and "no texting" is the only rule Yves established in our group, with her in mind. We nominated him as our mediator. "This isn't a patriarchal thing," I'd said to him about his boss title. "You're just better at keeping track." In a way we are more vulnerable without Julia. Is it friendship we're after? I wonder. Is that really what therapy is about?

"My husband won't let me have coffee," I interject, feeling the caffeine in my temples. "He read that it inhibits the ovaries.

He bought a $700 Vitamix juicer so I can live on a head of spinach reduced to a puddle of grit."

I try hard not to, but in a way I feel better than everyone else here, not because my troubles are fewer but my social standing makes my difficulties seem to pale against the others. Toby's a highly regarded veterinarian, and I'm an urban designer. My job is basically to provide the Toronto metro with my New York aesthetic, make the city more visually appealing. We live in a beautiful loft on King, with tons of natural light and access to everything on foot.

My problem, according to Julia, is chronic anxiety, mostly over the fact that I do not have a child. She told me it's the one thing I haven't been able to "acquire" easily, as if every pursuit in my life has come effortlessly. As if everything is something to acquire.

"Jesus," says Yves. He is French Canadian and seems to live on espresso, cigarettes, and sex. He is often dressed in sweatpants and sneakers—it's remarkable that he still looks smart; perhaps it's because he is sinewy and wears an expensive wool cap. "That's criminal," he says about my not being allowed caffeine, and we laugh. Yves and I are the most alike.

"What a douchebag," says Claire. "You've been trying for six years. It's not the java, for fuck's sake."

She swears like it's recreation, and we know it's one of the few ways she can be free. Sometimes when things are really stressful she'll go outside with Elena and smoke, and then go into the bathroom and throw up so she smells like vomit instead of nicotine. She doesn't wear a hijab, but her retaliations are so restrained against a culture that would stone her in certain circumstances. Sometimes I want to shake her. She is Dove-soap-like in color and grew up with weird Quaker parents, and the idea of her marrying Mustafa as rebellion seems too straightforward.

"What about you, E? You dreaming up a juicy Facebook status?" says Yves, calling Elena on her obvious boredom, and maintaining his job as mediator.

"I'm thinking of quitting music, going home to Calgary," Elena says. "Fucking the dog or whatever and reclaiming my silver spoon." Without the therapy group, Elena and I would never have crossed paths. Her parents are rich Italian immigrants who fashioned her into a *principessa*. She claims she's bipolar and has little imagination for what it might be like to be anyone else but her.

Still, I enjoy her. She is twenty-five and kind of nutty; she has a gorgeous singing voice, and the punchline is that she's addicted to some American country singer, Aaron Tippin, and has blatantly siphoned her parents' wealth to stalk him at concerts across the United States. At present she is trying to break up the guy's marriage or she'll off herself, she told us last time. Also, she has this tattoo of the Rolling Stones tongue on her neck and it makes me a little afraid of her.

I look down and Nedi's eyes have opened to a slant, and I quickly pick her up before Claire has a chance to notice. The baby is delicately warm yet solid against my silk blouse.

"Are you taking your meds?" I ask Elena. Some part of me wants to say things to turn her inside out.

"I totally need to up the dose," she says, looking at everyone, "don't you think?"

"Are you exercising?" Yves asks. "Why don't you run the lakeshore with me, it's a hoot."

"I'd rather pop a pill and rev up on Diet Pepsi."

Fair enough. We're all sick of role-playing with Elena to source some kernel of sadness in her childhood. She needs to get through her twenties is all. Her determination is admirable, but it shoots off in every direction. I wish I were still her age and knew what I know now. I'd have had ten babies by now.

"My father says he loves me whether I'm on *Canadian Idol* or not. I could work in one of his oil company offices," Elena says.

"Sure," Claire responds. "Put a gun in your mouth after a week in the warehouse." It's hard for us not to project. Claire takes on a motherly role, but her patience for Elena is about the length of a toothpick. Claire can only see Elena for the freedom she has, something she herself will never get back.

"Remember your mother sitting on the couch flipping through gossip rags and recipe books all day, freezing her butt off in Calgary," I tell her. "That's bleak. Head south. The clock is ticking."

I feel my chest tighten. I haven't told anyone, not even Toby, but I just found out that I'm not capable of having a child.

"I resent that, Eva," she says to me. "You're just bitter 'cause you wish you were Claire."

"That's a laugh," Claire says. "You mean it the other way around, right? Mustafa and I finally agreed that I won't talk, ever, around his friends." She's jumping right back into her problems. Good. The nerve of Elena.

"I showed a doctor buddy of his a blister on my finger, and Mustafa said it was disrespectful to offer a woman's hands. It's like farting, he said. So now I have tape over my mouth."

I snuggle into baby Nedi and the sweetness of her fine hair smells like roses, and I imagine her in the *Madeline* crib Toby and I bought at Pottery Barn a few years ago for the baby's room.

A little thing in the scale of life's suffering, eh? There's a baby's room we'll never need. So what? In the next moment I think Elena is right, that it's true. I wouldn't mind having Claire's life if it meant having children.

I say to her, "You deserve more, Claire. Stay at my house for a bit? We've got plenty of room."

She smiles and pats my arm. I feel a pang of desperation hoping she'll agree to come.

"In my defense, I told Toby he needed to work out less. Found out it hurts the sperm count," I offer, to try to loosen the grasp of the abject truth that has yet to sink in.

"Have you tried going on a date?" Yves says. "Putting on some 'come hither' boots, wearing something sexy?"

"Fuck you," I say, because we have done just that so many times.

"All right," he says. "Julia would say, 'Have you tried the C word?' Communication, honey."

"I pulled up the adoption site the other night. I want an Ethiopian baby. They're so unwanted. Self-righteous of me, right?"

But that's not how I feel. I dream about their beautiful brown skin and soft curls and would give any amount of money to be on a plane to Addis Ababa. It's fear that holds me back or something else. Maybe I'm just like Toby. I see so many happy white parents with Asian children and I always imagine they know something I don't.

"Why don't you do it yourself?" says Elena, her big blue eyes on me, as if she's Bianca Balti, all Italian youth and confidence. She has it in for me today. "You're a coward, eh? That's what's stopping you. I never knew how I was getting to Nashville for Aaron's last concert but I made it, didn't I?"

"Who's the one moving back to Calgary? You make no sense, Elena." My cheeks are warm. I count to ten in my head and breathe out.

"Listen, your husband is a vet and won't let you have a dog. That says it all."

"It's against condo rules. You know that."

"That's an excuse," Elena says, and isn't backing down. "Toby runs your life."

"Hey. Enough. You can't talk to me like that. Yves, tell her."

Suddenly I'm the child in this mess, and I need Yves's rescue. I wonder if it's in my face or my voice that I think Toby is leaving me soon. If Elena only knew.

"You're all leash," he told me last week. "I can't be comfortable in my own condo anymore. You've got it rigged so our failure is staring at us from every angle."

"Let's call it, darlings," Yves says, and he gets up abruptly, kisses me and the baby on both cheeks, and makes his way around the table to hug Elena and Claire. I think we all realize suddenly that he didn't get to spill, but that is part of Yves's problem—avoidance.

"I'll get this one," he says, takes the check, and is gone.

Back at my apartment, Claire falls asleep on the sofa with a cashmere throw over her legs. At the last minute she'd agreed to come round to rest and let me play with Nedi. I called the office and told them I wouldn't be in for the rest of the day. I am down on the Persian rug with Nedi.

From the bookshelf I take a squishy, brightly colored square block. I roll it along the soft rug. Nedi crawls along and grabs hold of the block, then hands it to me, and laughs. I move the block to another part of the carpet, and she crawls over to it, then brings it back again, smiling. She's delightful.

I think if Toby saw me with her right now, he'd get it. He'd see me like he used to. I move the block again, and Nedi makes her way to it. We do this over and over. I am bewitched by her.

The keys to Claire's Volvo dangle out of her diaper bag. If I'm really quiet and she stays sleeping, I'll fetch her other children at the preschool. I could bring them back here and make a big meal. I've got enough vegetables to put in a pot with bouillon and chicken, and then we might play games by the fireplace; I'll make popcorn and we'll giggle and talk. The older girls will want to play in my bedroom, and I'll get out my big bucket of scarves and we'll dance around with that Putumayo kids' music playing on my iPhone.

Nedi cackles a laugh when she bonks herself on the nose with the block. Her laugh wakes Claire. She is up like a shot, and there's drool on the down throw pillow. Claire grabs her coat and keys and slips into her shoes without bothering to fit her heels in properly.

"Fucking shit," Claire says. "I'm late for carpool."

She hugs me with Nedi already on her hip.

"Why'd you let me sleep?" She doesn't wait for an answer and swings open the apartment door. I follow her into the hallway.

"I'm going to make a roast chicken," I say. "I'll start on it right away. It'll be fun. We'll all eat together."

"Oh, Eva, I can't," she sighs. "My girls need to see their

father. They miss him." She comes back toward me and gives me another hug. A pity hug, I know, but I take it.

"I'll see you next week, okay?"

I am unable to speak. I hear the ding of the elevator and they go in and the door closes.

Those children miss that father. I leave my apartment door open and lie on the couch exactly the way Claire had. I look out the big bay window and imagine Nedi is still there on the rug, playing. I visualize that I have someone just like her to worry about and to make me feel harried and overwhelmed with what there is to do. It is a lovely haze to be in.

Later, I go into the kitchen and take down the instant espresso I've hidden behind the paper towels in the cabinet above the refrigerator. I boil water and make the coffee good and strong. At the computer I open the adoption site and fill out the registration page in both our names, forging answers for Toby because we haven't had the conversation. I know I have no chance if there aren't two parents on the form. That's clear.

I'll tell him tonight. And I'm pretty sure it's the thing that will make him leave me. I complete the form quickly, and another comes up saying I'll hear about an interview in two to three months, possibly sooner. I sit on the couch looking out at the rush-hour traffic as dusk moves in. The clouds fill quickly with shades of charcoal, rain hits the pane of glass, and it is evening.

I hear footsteps from the hallway. It's Toby. I shut my eyes and pretend to be asleep.

ZEE HOUSE

The idea of living together came to Paula and Genie on one of their annual canoe trips to the Kootenays, a three-hour drive west of Calgary, in the Canadian Rockies. This was before Paula's divorce, when she complained about Todd mostly to make Genie laugh, the way friends complain to each other about their husbands. In the canoe that day, they admired the mountains and spoke not of their troubles but of their ideals. It was the kind of imagining that can only happen on holiday.

Wouldn't it be grand to live with your best friend in a well-designed home, combining assets and sharing some of the best comforts of a marriage, without the trouble of a man? They'd joked about it for years, coming up with ever more elaborate plans: a lap pool in the basement; a greenhouse, an atrium with an elm shooting up through the center of the glass ceiling; an outdoor shower; a dance floor, yes, a dance floor.

It was exhilarating to dream it up.

Remarkably, they made it happen.

They split the cost of a corner lot in an upscale neighborhood on the edge of the downtown core. Genie was the one to put the fire behind it. Once she got an idea in her head, look out. An ex-boyfriend of hers, an architect, worked tirelessly to get her progressive ideas incorporated into their dream *green* home, and once it was finally to her liking, she convinced Tony Fresno, the builder, that he'd be established as the go-to guy for eco-homes, and they got a significant reduction on the price. At cost, Tony said.

Paula trusted Genie implicitly, and with good reason. Genie got them a grant from the Alberta Urban Development Fund for building the first energy-efficient home in the Deerfoot region. Incredible.

Before they moved in, the *Observer* had Genie on the front

cover of its weekend magazine, atop the steps of their recycled-lumber porch, resurfaced with the soles of crushed-up Nike tennis shoes. The article made no mention of the platonic setup the women had, only the superior environmental design, the state-of-the-art geothermal heating system, the photovoltaic solar panels, the ultra-efficient loft insulation, and how the placement of the windows and doors maximizes ventilation—"breezeways" as Genie calls them. Truly, the article was a promotional package, a vignette about a successful, forward-thinking go-getter, which is all true about Genie, and she garnered many new clients from it.

This is the kind of thing Len, Paula's therapist (another ex of Genie's) wants for Paula. He tells her to be more outspoken and direct, essentially more like her best friend. Len has her punch a heavy bag that hangs in the corner of his office overlooking Fourth Avenue. One night she and Genie conspired over a bottle of chardonnay and steamed mussels, and by the end of it Paula put on one of Genie's power suits and did an impression of Genie's fierce business voice as if she were talking to Len. Genie howled.

"He's still in love with you," Paula told her. "The man should be paying me for our sessions."

They are two mature single women living together. They call their house *Zee House*, because of its shape but also because it is *the one*, the original, *zee* place to be. One rectangle per woman, each with her own bright bedroom and bathroom, study, and private garden. They meet in the middle of the Z when they feel like company. They sit on their modern and comfy white couch for movies and share meals in the open-concept kitchen.

It works out that Paula does the cooking while Genie does her part shopping for provisions on her way home from the office and taking care of the koi pond and Japanese garden. This arrangement suits them well. One never measures what the other is doing. That's one of their rules—no measuring tit for tat. And no meddling.

That was before Dan, Genie's grown son, arrived at their door with his pillow. They'd had eight glorious months, but now Dan is in the house. All the time. His wife had confessed she was in love with the French teacher at the elementary school where she teaches PE. Couldn't have scripted it more cliché. So, for weeks the two women coddled Dan, and let him lie there in the common area on the slipcovered couch and watch television, bringing him cups of tea and bowls of noodles and broth, fluffing the down duvet, and trying to get him to talk, to eat.

But now Dan has become a kind of paradigm of male depression: an inert, heavy, insistent presence. Even considering what he has been through and how similar their betrayals, Paula finds herself angry at him somehow, for this very similarity. She's surprised herself with her visceral aversion toward his company. All her pent-up anger about Todd's dalliances was being redirected at Dan. Len has said so.

"Just rest this on your tongue," Paula heard Genie say one day, when she came into the kitchen to grab a yogurt. Genie was standing beside Dan's chair with a piece of barbeque steak on a fork. Good god. *You'd feed your son from your breasts if you could,* Paula wanted to say but didn't. She wanted to take the man by the shoulders and rattle him.

"I don't want to eat, Ma," he said, turning his body from her. "I'm not gonna starve."

"Why don't we go to a movie like we used to," Genie said and tossed the fork with the meat into the kitchen sink.

"We've been to two movies together. Ever," Dan said.

"That's not true."

"Just leave me alone," he said, and went back to his station on the couch.

Paula couldn't help it. She followed Genie as she went toward her half of the house and stopped at the edge of the carpet that divides the common area from what was officially Genie's side, then she called out Genie's name. No answer. She peeked her head in and walked a little way down the hallway. Why not? All the rules had changed since Dan upset their bliss.

"What is it?" Genie asked.

"You doing okay?"

"Fine."

"Does he want her back, Genie?" Paula asked.

"He's begging her."

"Has he quit his job?"

"He's on extended leave. He has one focus at the moment."

"You know, it might be time for some of that tough love you gave me when I was going through it."

"You're still going through it," Genie said.

Paula gave her that look. She'd had a continuing annoyance at Genie for acting like the authority on everything since Dan arrived. They'd lost the sense of spontaneity in the house.

"Can I drive him there?" she said and paused. "To work? Or to see her?"

"It's not as simple as that, Paula."

"Will she see you?"

"She's the asshole and he's the innocent one," Genie said. "Let's stay out of it."

Paula knew her best friend well enough to know that she had closed up, like a clam, like a man, and she'd have to wait for a better time to say anything more. There was nothing to do but turn around and retrace her steps through the house, past the lump on the couch, and back to the quiet of her own space. She lay flat on her bed and placed a rose quartz stone under her blouse, on her heart, and attempted a chant with her eyes closed.

Oh, how she missed when it was just the two of them.

The women met fifteen years ago at one of Paula and Todd's swank dinner parties. Genie was dating a colleague of Todd's at the law firm and the two women wound up in the kitchen talking about their children. Paula's oldest, Scott, had been on the same hockey team as Dan in eighth grade. At the time, Todd wanted to move into a bigger, even more ornamental house, and for weeks Genie drove Paula all over the richest parts of Calgary looking for the right address.

In the end, Genie, who would have made a packet on the deal, helped Paula realize the truth—that she didn't want a bigger house, that perhaps she wanted less. She coached Paula through every step of telling Todd this, and then she coached her through opening her eyes to Todd's penchant for administrative assistants.

Genie had divorced early and started out as a single mom and receptionist at Dennis Handy Real Estate Company. She worked her way toward her real estate license, and became a workhorse, always at the ready, always the last to leave—and she built a steady clientele. She is a bright woman with blond wispy hair and pretty nails and blue eye shadow, and she has a way of talking that draws everyone in. Genie has plenty of men after her, of course, and keeps one on the go. But once they inch toward the threshold of boyfriend, it fizzles quickly. It's like watching a wet finger to a lit match.

Now Paula feels sleepy reading the massage therapy manuals from the library. She's been trying to ready herself for the class Genie encouraged her to enroll in at the community college. She needs a strong cup of tea and can't avoid the kitchen. Dan is splayed out in the great room watching another cooking show. She sits on a barstool eating Triscuits from the box, looking out at the koi pond and waiting for the kettle to boil, her back to the television. She hears that gorgeous Italian woman making sauces: marinara, artichoke pesto, white carbonara, all the colors of the Italian flag. Paula can't help but swing around and watch. Giada—that's the woman's name—seems to be on the verge of dipping herself into the deep pot.

"She disgusts me," Paula says to no one, and is surprised at how mean-spirited the comment sounds.

"Yes, but will she spill any of it on her white top?" says Dan, and she laughs out loud.

"You're hoping for it."

"Sure."

"Do cooking shows cure a broken heart?"

Dan sits up abruptly and mutes the TV.

"Not so far." And he looks sad. Oh, brother.

"You could try something more manly, like race car driving or porn."

"You don't know anything about me," he says.

"I'm sorry," she says. "That was unfair. I'm just a crotchety old lady. Ignore me."

He sits up straight and props a pillow behind his back and turns the TV off.

"Please, put it back on. I've just come for my tea. It's not bothering me."

"I think I need to go."

She wants nothing more than this. "What are you talking about?"

"You've put up with me long enough. Wouldn't you say?"

"Your mother has loved having you here." She suddenly feels sorry for him.

"And you?"

"Everything's fine." Paula sits on the ottoman beside the couch. She feels as if she owes him an explanation for all that she's felt about him. Suddenly she wants to cry. "Look, I went through this. It just takes time. I'm just being grumpy. Don't give me a second thought."

"You're the boss," he says, completely misunderstanding her intentions.

"I'm just saying, this too shall pass."

"Whatever you say." He gets up and looks at her with something like fear in his eyes. It does look like fear—or wariness. Then he sits back down.

"Do you—do you want to talk about your marriage?"

"No," she says, and remembers to smile. "Do you?"

"God, no," he says.

And they are both smiling.

"Maybe you need a buddy," Paula tells him. "Someone, a guy, you can talk to the way I talk to your mom."

"You're a real trooper to put up with her."

"Your mother? She saved my life."

"That's her thing," he says. "She saves people. Always looking for her next project."

"Hopefully I'm a keeper."

"I think you are," Dan says. "You guys are so different. You're cool and she's got an agenda."

"All of a sudden you've got opinions." Paula's face gets warm. "I don't mean anything by it. It's just a mother-son thing. You can never please them."

"She thinks the world of you, Dan."

"You can't imagine what my childhood was like."

"I know all about it. I'm sure it was hard without a father around."

Get over yourself, you're a grown person, she wants to say.

"Mom overdid it, hoping I wouldn't notice. I was just a kid. I just wanted her to relax a little. And when I got older—my teens—we didn't get along. She ever tell you about it?"

"She's my best friend—but she doesn't dwell on the past."

"It sucks that she's bailing me out."

"She bailed me out too." Paula can't tell if she seems motherly to him or if he is looking at her the way a man looks at a woman, taking in her shape.

"You're amazing," he says, as if she has passed some test. "I think the world of you."

"You like cranky women?"

"I have a long history of devotion to cranky women."

"Well, that's good. We'll be friends." A silence follows.

"Good night, Dan," she says, getting up.

"Welcome back to the land of the living," and she taps the side of his arm.

Back in her room, she feels strange. She sits up in bed and sips her tea. Everything seems unsteady. It takes her back to the end with Todd, an awful night, not even a year ago, the final straw—with Ariel, his client. A nice girl, everyone said, and it wasn't her fault, knowing Todd, but he had been so sloppy, as if he wanted to get caught. The idea of one more disloyalty made

Paula so crazy that she drove his MG through the garage door. She can't imagine now that she did such a thing. That she was capable of it.

Genie happened to pull into the driveway a few minutes later, and got her out of the car and to the emergency room. She had to have stitches in her forehead and wore a neck brace for six weeks. Genie took care of things. She was ruthless, and helped Paula make huge withdrawals from Todd's bank account and credit cards, then created separate accounts, and Paula sat there like a stone. A lost puppy.

It is true that her relationship with Genie has brought her so much closer to the person she wants to be. Strong and detached. More active. She's going to be a certified massage therapist—well, she hasn't exactly signed up yet. Across the mirror in her bathroom, in cherry lipstick, are the words: *I am the boss of me.* She says this out loud every time she sees it. "A mantra," Len calls it. "I am the boss of me. I am the boss of me." She gets louder and feels her power and sometimes the thought of freedom delights her so much that she laughs, a real belly laugh.

Len speaks in terms of *listening to her inner voice* and *clearing her chakras*, instead of slogging through her relationship with her mother, for instance. Genie tells her it's the better way, so much more forward-thinking, more light than dark.

Paula doesn't want to think anymore. She gets up and takes half of an Ativan and waits for sleep to come.

Morning was always a sacred time for the women. There was no talking, only slow movements, and no loud noises or domestic questions. They'd exchange a simple "good morning" and then go back to their rooms and their separate morning rituals. For Genie it's exercise, the bike for thirty minutes, stretching, and then a shower and business. Paula tries her balance breathing with the help of a guided meditation on YouTube. It usually lasts ten minutes and then she'll write two pages in her flower journal, the way Len has instructed her to.

But this morning, she finds Dan dressed when she gets her morning coffee. Dressed and cheerful. The TV is off. He announces that he's making Greek eggs for everyone. He saw it on the Aphrodite Cooking Show, and he's wearing Paula's denim apron.

"Lightly scrambled eggs," he says, "with spinach and goat cheese folded in, then baked."

"I'd love some, son." Genie beams, clearly thrilled at his newfound energy.

"No thanks," Paula says.

"Oh, come on." Genie is clearly disappointed. "When was the last time we had a handsome man make us breakfast?"

Paula half-sits on a chair at the parlor table and sips her coffee while Genie rushes into her part of the house to get a third seat for the small round table.

"Mom, don't make her eat. You've got to learn to take no for an answer."

"This is Paula. Sometimes she doesn't know what's best for her."

"Now you're insulting our guest." He could have meant it as a joke.

"Guest?" Genie says. She shakes her head, as if the whole exchange is too trivial for any other reaction.

"I'll let you all decide if I'm being slighted," Paula says, and gets up.

"You're always doing that, Mom. You don't realize it but you offend people."

"You're the one who said *guest*!"

Now they are all avoiding eye contact.

"Look," Paula says. "I just don't eat much in the morning. You know that, Genie." She smiles at her friend.

"We usually don't speak until noon," Genie tells her son, as if he hasn't figured this out by now. The women exchange a knowing glance. This creates a closeness, something they haven't felt since Dan's arrival. Paula's head is foggy from the Ativan but she makes her way around the small table and hugs Genie, and since Dan is standing there above his mother, she surprises herself and gives him a small peck on the cheek. He takes hold of her upper arms and pulls her toward him for an embrace. It's gentle but there's a quickness to his movements that makes Paula sink into him and let him direct the end of the hug.

She's glad she has the excuse of seeing Len later this morning. She excuses herself and has the childlike idea that a swim before her appointment will make her feel better. When she comes out of the bathroom in her swimsuit with a towel around her shoulders, Dan is there, sitting on her bed. In her part of the *Zee*.

"How did the eggs turn out?" she says, trying to sound casual.

"Well, not as well as George the Greek's, but Mom praised them to high heaven."

She looks at him. "Do you need something?"

"No. I just came in to say hi."

"Hi," she says. "I'm going for a swim now."

"Can I come and watch?"

"I hope you're kidding."

"I'm trying to get off the couch."

"Why don't you take a walk?"

"I'd rather talk with you," he says, and moves closer to where she stands against her dresser. "Or not, if you're too busy."

"Some other time," she says. And she walks into the closet to get her goggles.

"I really loved talking to you last night. I feel like you're a contemporary, you know."

"We both got cheated on. We've got that in common."

"A couple of castoffs, eh."

"I'm sorry you feel like that," she says.

"I'm starting to feel like it was the best thing that happened to me."

"That's progress," she says and hurries out of the room and along the glassed-in corridor, where she can see the day opening up into sunshine.

He's behind her and she hopes he'll veer right, but instead

he comes down the stairwell. *I am the boss of me*, she thinks. She turns to him halfway down.

"Listen, I'd like to swim by myself, if you don't mind." She's breathing heavily, and evidently he notices.

"Don't get flustered. I was just hoping for some company."

"I'm going to be swimming."

"Hey, I don't want to piss you off. I think you're beautiful. That's all I wanted to tell you."

"Oh," she says, and holds on to the railing, feeling unpleasantly flattered. She hears the door close quietly at the top of the stairs.

Sitting on the edge of the lap pool, she moves her feet in circles in the water. All she can think of is getting out of the house, and away. She knows she won't swim. She tiptoes back up the stairs and along the corridor and locks her door, then gets into the shower.

She stays out all day and intentionally returns home late. The house is quiet and it's odd now without the sound of voices coming from the television. With the keys still in her hand, she flicks the light on in the kitchen and is aware of the possibility of strangers in the house. She moves into the great room and sees the sliding glass doors open. She walks out to the garden and finds Dan sitting on the bench under the lit candelabra, drinking a glass of white wine. On the table beside him is an assortment of small dishes. It all looks untouched, but the wine bottle is half empty.

"Is your mother home?" she asks him.

"She's showing houses."

"You seem to be managing okay."

"Can I pour you some wine?"

"I'd just be crashing the party," she says. But his face looks different somehow, softer, and less serious. She watches while he pours the wine and licks the edge of the bottle where a little has dripped.

She has a quick thrill in the moment. Without quite thinking about it—except as a heightening of all her senses—a terrible curiosity seizes her. She takes the glass from him and he offers a tour of the dishes he's prepared. A tapas menu from George the Greek on television: dolmades, taramosalata, spanakopita, hummus, and grilled meat on skewers. It all looks delicious. The truth is, anyway, she's hungry and it has not been a very productive day. The session with Len left her feeling flat. She has decided that Dan is just in need of some attention. He's Genie's son, after all. They eat together on the bench with the pleasant breezes under the archway. They talk openly about their failed marriages and he seems to want to know every detail of hers. She's aware that when she talks about it, she's using her talking-to-Len voice, filtering what the other person will think, before speaking.

"Were the two of you still intimate by the end of it?" he asks.

"I'm not going to talk about that," she tells him.

"Simple question."

"And that's my simple answer."

"How about you and Mom?" he says, and he has a look in his eyes that says this is his real question.

Slowly she puts her glass down and laughs, then sits back.

"I'm just joking."

"You know, I was really enjoying you for a minute, Dan."

"But?"

"You are unpredictable. I'll give you that."

"You don't trust me."

"Exactly."

She feels the wine at her temples and at the base of her throat and she turns to say something but doesn't. She gets up, not wanting to keep the conversation going.

"Well, I trust you," he says. "We're having fun, aren't we?"

She walks up the few porch steps and opens the sliding glass doors. He follows her. Inside, keeping her back to him, she takes a glass from the cupboard and pushes the button on the refrigerator to dispense filtered water. She feels trapped in her own home. Frozen. She sips the water and leans against the fridge, in disbelief. He's standing there in the doorway looking at her and there is no hesitation about his intention. As he comes toward her she braces herself, not knowing what she wants. She feels both excited and repulsed. He puts one hand against the fridge and leans in very close to her. His other hand lifts her chin, and her body tightens. His rough cheek touches the side of her neck and she feels the pleasure move down her back. She hears the front door opening and he is kissing her ear.

"I'm home," Genie calls and Dan spins away from her and is out the patio door. Genie's heels move quickly into the kitchen, dropping her heavy handbag and a stack of Redbox movies on the counter. Paula attempts a look of calm, one that gives nothing away. But Genie, who's smiling her professional smile, one that doesn't show any teeth, barely glances at her.

"Where is he?" Genie mouths.

She points to the open glass doors and Genie spots her son. Paula stays put against the refrigerator and listens to mother and son. She hears Genie's delight that her son has been cooking again, the best sign that he's on the mend. She hears the familiar words *You're getting your power back.*

No, Paula thinks, he's just after your roommate. She shudders at the thought that she and Dan are the same to Genie. The walking wounded, the kept ones, and Genie has been the saving presence, nurse, teacher, motivator, mother.

Paula passes through the rooms back to her half of the house and almost trips on one of Dan's shoes, which is sticking out from the back of the couch, like the clutter of a little boy.

In her room, she wants to pick up anything that will take her someplace else and make her feel useful. She opens the anatomy book and concentrates on the Latin and Greek words, naming the parts of the body. She says them aloud.

"Capillus. Oculus. Auricula. Nasus. Lingua."

Maybe it's simple. Dan is just a guy, after all. Maybe he's truly attracted to her as herself and values her opinions; maybe also he's just hurt and confused. It comes to her that Genie is just as fragile, just as vulnerable, with her ever-present need to control. It all makes sense now.

And maybe, just maybe, Paula will finally trust herself and learn to listen to her own inner voice. She walks around her room and puts her hand on her armoire, her dresser, and then her dressing-table mirror—the furniture she chose herself: her things, her life.

LONG DIVISION

Kenya, Africa

Africa! Nine thousand miles from Portland where I live. My wayward son Tim walks toward me with four tall, dark-as-midnight women. He has seen me, I'm quite sure of it, but nothing about his gait changes. He arrives at the tent and doesn't say a word or make any motion toward me. The thirty or so Kenyan women standing around are curious, and openly gawking at me. Tim indicates what he wants people to do. They set up two wobbly card tables in the corner of the tent and arrange the women in lines. I walk over to my son.

"Hello," he says, and there is no surprise in his face that his father has traveled around the world to see him. I've come all this way. And no surprise.

"I can't believe I've tracked you down," I say and hold my arms out for a hug. We manage it, but it's awkward. I pull away before tears come. I don't think he notices.

"Well, I'm happy to see you," he tells me, as I say again, "I can't believe I found you."

My son is like the counselor in a camp you've never seen the likes of walking around with his clipboard and his preppy shorts, and the wide hat with the loose string down his chest. Any second, I expect that he'll forage a whistle out of his pocket and blow.

Outside the tent I follow him and watch as he orchestrates the various groups; some are weaving baskets, and over to one side there's an outdoor cooker where four women stand over two large metal pots. Steam rises above their heads.

I realize that I'm seeing my son as he is in the world, with no reference to me at all. Of course, he's doing what he does best, helping people. Tim is all pathos, while I am logos; I have a very logical mind. I'm a businessman, now in retirement. I have always believed that you have to pay close attention to what the other guy is thinking; Tim just anticipates what others might *need.* I am proud of Tim but have I actually told him? It occurs to me that I haven't.

I'm just standing there watching him do the work of organizing things in the camp, or whatever this is. He was always so much his mother's boy, and he all but raised his sister, Maddy. When he was little I helped him with math problems once. Once. His mother talked about that a lot in the weeks before she died; the only instance of my ever being a father to him. The famous instance.

It's Maddy I've come to see Tim about.

Arriving in this country last week was like stepping off an elevator into an oven. When I was much younger, I was hungry for travel, for looking at things. But never this, not Africa. Not even once.

When Tim pauses to drink from his canteen I say, "I'm here to ask you to come home."

He shakes his head, swallowing. "I thought for a second you were here to help. You're retired now, right?" He makes his way over to a rickety chair under an acacia tree, and I follow him again. He turns back to look at me. "It's a ridiculous thought, I know." It appears this group of women had been waiting for him. They plant themselves at his feet like kids at a story reading. He seems relieved to return to the important matter at hand.

"It's your sister," I say, imposing on him as he's ready to begin attending to the group. "She's gone into one of her unreachable places again. I thought if she could see you, she'd get through it. Just a short visit, Tim."

"How did you find me?" he asks.

"One week and I'd have you right back here."

"You wasted your money, Dad."

He motions for the first woman to come up. She has a baby with her, a tiny thing who is nursing right there in the open. The woman looks beyond child-bearing years. Tim greets her warmly. There is little space between us and I feel like an intruder so I move back.

"I walk five kilometers," the woman tells my son and moves even closer to him. "Then I ride the bus for an hour before I reach my workplace. There are four nurses but I am alone on duty with around seventy to one hundred patients, mostly HIV."

"The other nurses can't relieve you?" Tim asks.

"They are too afraid of infection. Many times the worker doesn't show up so I am staying twenty-four hours." The woman's face doesn't change while she talks; there seems very little feeling in it. She's just telling facts, like someone cataloging crimes.

"I'm so sorry," Tim says. He gives her the bottle of water he's holding, probably his own. "Can I offer you a meal?"

Tim stands up. He hands her pieces of paper, coupons of some sort, and she continues to the next station where there is a table with a large vessel where another volunteer is serving food.

"My husband is furious." Another woman is up now talking to Tim, the next in line, and her eyes are filled with sadness. She looks down at the brown earth.

"You're safe with us," he says.

"I am here for the others," she tells him.

He leads her to a group sitting on a small patch of grass. They wear brightly colored yet slightly faded cloth, some worn as skirts and some as dresses, some tied at the back of the neck. Their heads are covered in multicolored scarves. They are beautiful women from a distance. But up close their teeth are yellow and rotting and lines crease their faces. A few of them are laughing but to me it sounds like rain on a tin roof. I go over to them and their expressions turn vinegary.

"How are you, Mzungu, father of Tim?" one of them says.

Mzungu means white man. I know at least this from my time in Mombasa.

When I ask them about themselves they are guarded: God is good to them, they say; they are glad to see me. I'm amazed at how clear and unaccented their English is. "How are you? How are you?" I say, nodding, but I don't really want to know the answer. I pretend I am walking over to a lone plumeria tree. I slow down and get a better spot to hear them.

"I have eight grandchildren, from two to fourteen years, all living with me. I have six children of my own and four are dead. One of my sons is now very sick and god willing, he will be well. My husband left us a long time ago. I believe he's still alive."

I realize, my god, they're swapping stories. They're sitting in a circle now and each one takes the others through her own corner of hell.

It's awful but I'm distracted. I need Tim to listen to me.

"You're the only one who can do this," I say to him about Maddy. He doesn't respond; he keeps moving. One of the young women holds a steaming bowl out to me proudly. "It's a cassava vegetable paste made of maize flour. Delicious," she says. It's old people, living-in-a-facility food, overcooked mush but I take it and thank her. I don't want to be rude; I take a seat with them all next to Tim, on the hard earth, and it's deeply uncomfortable for me.

The sky is so vast it's disturbing, and the landscape is a big wasteland of dust.

"You've always been there for her—you're the only one who can reach her."

It's true. Tim has been more of a parent to Maddy than I ever have, and he must come home and he knows it. This is between us now, but he isn't looking at me. "She needs you, man."

"She's been depressed before," he says. "She gets herself out of these funks one way or another."

"She says you've abandoned her."

He smirks. "You know, she should wake up, get out of her tiny bubble." It's strange: here he is, saying the very thing I've always said to him about her. The very thing he would profess to hate about my pragmatic way of looking at things.

His mind is in the present and his life is here now; it's clear his very privileged life back home is now a small fraction of who he has become. "What we're trying to do first," he says to me, "is make these women understand that they don't have to accept the life they've been handed." He takes a clawful of what the woman called *ugali,* the porridge stuff, and puts it between his teeth. "We're trying to show them," he goes on, chewing, "that they can choose a different way. They can come to the center and make baskets and be part of a community."

"I know what you think of me," I say. I hadn't known I would say it but he isn't even listening.

He goes on. "It's like a witness protection plan without the protection. The witnesses are taught to stand up for themselves. It creates a great circle of community."

"Catherine is with her," I say, with the intention of getting a rise out of him. Catherine is Tim's ex. "She and Maddy are great pals, as you know. Until Maddy started living between the bathroom and the kitchen." He is unfazed by the comment.

"Does Catherine need money—is that it?"

"What the hell does that say about your sister?"

"No—it's what I'm saying about Catherine." After a pause, he adds, "Maddy's a grown-up. She can handle herself. She knows I love her."

"Man, she won't talk to me. Hasn't much at all—and you know this—since your mother and I—and then your mother— that's the thing. I want to get past it. How many times do I have to say I take the blame for everything? I came all this way, Tim. I found you."

"You're not listening to me," he says. "They're all dying, here, Pops. One after another after another. A full third of the population."

"I know. This would just be for a couple of weeks. One

week is fine. You could settle her a little, bring her out of it. She's always responded to you."

He's barely listening. It's like he almost finds Maddy's situation, and me, for that matter, annoying. He starts talking to people at the table, away from me.

"I tell them, you know, stick together. I tell them they don't have to have intercourse with their husbands, like the culture says they do." He looks over at me and I see it in his eyes, his wish for me to leave. "I tell them to stay with a friend, run away. We're working on building a community space," he says. "They believe there's only one direction."

"Your sister needs to hear from you. You know that."

"I've got this to do, here."

It comes to me that in his mind I am more outsider than father. "Listen," I say. "You're a better man than me, son. You are. You were always the one she turned to for help."

He just stares.

"Just one week and I'll send you right back here," I say. "First class."

He gazes ahead to the edge of the hill where the women are walking together.

"Please, son."

And then he starts laughing. He fights it, putting a hand over his mouth. "You came all this way. You—all those miles. Did you think you could just collect me like some lost little kid? Maddy's fine. She's got her apartment and her acting and her friendship with Catherine; these people have nothing. You found me—now go and find her."

"One week," I say, pleading.

Later, he's hugging people, thanking them and packing up his supplies in a small Renault hatchback. Heading off, my son, the savior. I catch myself calculating how much money I should leave for him. I catch myself, again, thinking about money.

One week. That was all I asked of him.

HOW I BECAME A BANKER

I made a promise to myself when I was twelve that no matter what, I'd make a shitload of money. I was a third of the age I am now, and my father and I were driving south on the I-90 to Salamanca, New York, a valley near the Holiday Valley ski resort, where he'd just bought an old ranch house. The sudden real estate purchase and the overnight invitation were intimidating. We were so often on the verge of losing everything, and he'd spent little time with me or my two younger sisters.

We stopped for gas, and when my father came out from paying, I saw his breath in thin clouds against the collar of his coat. He started pumping and knocked on the back window. "Hon, get me a coffee. Blond and sweet," he said. It was winter-dark out, and we were in the United States of America, not the small town on the Canadian side of the border where I grew up.

I looked around and saw a few metalheads standing by a motorcycle and a harried-looking lady in the passenger seat of a beat-up Chevy. In the GasMart I poured the coffee, wanting to get the milk and sugar just right. He had given me a US twenty-dollar bill during the drive—as something to do, talk about money—I think he thought it would delight me. I was the "saver" in the family, and Dad joked that I'd had a bank account since birth. I eyed a 100 Grand chocolate bar, my favorite *only-in-America* bar, but I didn't pick it up. I paid for the coffee and counted out the change and put it in my pocket.

Back at the car, my father turned the gas cap with one hand, keeping the other warm in his coat pocket. His jeans hung on his chicken legs, and my mother often joked that his wallet gave him a lopsided ass. As sure as I knew anything in life, I could count on my father's clogs; the heavy-heeled Dutch kind were the only shoes he ever wore, and Eddie in the back shop of our family furniture store added two inches of rubber to the bottoms of every pair. A short Italian guy, my father, with a healthy dose of the short-man syndrome.

"Wait till you see this place, Lydia," he said. "It's majestic. Isn't that a lovely word? *Majestic.* Say it."

"Majestic," I said, always doing what I was told.

"It's a diamond in the rough. Kind of like me, don't you think?"

"Absolutely. You're a diamond in the rough, Dad." Building up his ego was part of my daughterly duties. But he'd always been a shiny diamond to me, the kind of guy they don't make anymore. "Straight from an Elmore Leonard novel," I'd say to colleagues over lunch on casual Fridays. "A gangster look-alike with chutzpah," I'd tell them.

Lyd, you're the one I'll tell all my secrets to. I must have been ten when he said it to me the first time. It was a Sunday, the only day our furniture shop closed, and we were working in his coveted rose garden after church, pulling weeds. I was thrilled he wanted to tell me things. It took years to understand that his confiding in me would be more of a burden than a gift.

The breakup with our mother had been awful. Dad got careless with his affairs, and our mother finally kicked him out when it was a friend of hers, another nurse at the hospital where she worked.

Buying the weekend place, god knows how, made it so my younger sisters and I would see Dad someplace other than the nurse's tiny duplex. As we went south on that barren highway that night and he drank his blond coffee, I understood it was his attempt to make the separation with our mother easier. But I could see the worry in his face. Business was bad. He laughed about the creditors calling our home phone. "All of them fuckin' idiots," he said, and at the time I believed him. He convinced us that these vendors who sent him to collections had betrayed him somehow, even though he had their furniture and hadn't paid for it.

"This milky toast guy from the electric company came and took the goddamn heater. Eddie had to hold me back. I would have slit the guy's throat," he said as we pulled into the Anchor Bar. "Let's get a bite."

"Jesus, Dad," I said. "You'll freeze to death."

He laughed. "Nah, I've got plenty of layers."

We ordered beef on wicks and a dozen clams casino, with hot sauce on the side. I remember that we ate ravenously. My father drank a pitcher of Michelob and teased the thick-lipped waitress. "Keep your eye on her," he said, pointing at me. "She can toss 'em back."

"She takes after her daddy," the waitress said, as if it were gallant for a tween to guzzle. This was his schtick.

"What's your name, hon?"

For my entire life, I swear, he'd asked every waitress this question—a game, and he had the controls.

"Tiffany," she said. "Rhymes with epiphany."

"Wow, that's a ten-dollar word," he quipped back.

"A lot more where that came from." Tiffany smiled, flirting with him right there in front of me. She had curly blond hair, the kind made with fat rollers and never brushed out.

"Can I get a virgin Bloody Mary, please," I said, finally, to indicate that I'd seen her kind before, many, many times.

When we arrived at the chalet as we came to call it, I stayed in the car with the high beams bright and watched him struggle with the lock. Once inside, he switched on the lights and turned on the furnace. He sent me around the side of the house to gather wood, and we built a fire together while the snow fell outside the huge bay window. It really was majestic. This became a ritual we would reenact for many years with my sisters, and later with my longtime boyfriend, Lou.

My father, an explorer in his heart and mind, would set out from the chalet at daybreak with a can of Anheuser-Busch in his coat pocket and wander for hours through the trees. "I wonder what the poor people are doing," he'd say, laughing. When he returned, he was happy and ready to make us all steak and eggs.

That first night, I remember I brought him the full bottle of Jim Beam, as he'd asked me to, then I set up the backgammon board and put on his favorite Enya CD. I lost the first game, and he sang in loud hums to the wispy music. Winning, even at something as small as a board game, always put him at ease. "I'm the current reigning champ," he'd announced, taking a happy swig. A win was a win for my father. Being a good sport was for "chumps," for people who wanted a cutout life. "Show me a good loser," he would say, "and I'll show you a loser." Even as his marriage failed, even with the constant threat of losing everything, he could imagine it all away in a moment of light.

I'd give anything for that gene now. I am constantly three steps ahead, expecting the worst. It's funny—I've got a healthy portfolio and retirement plan, and yet I'm constantly afraid of the future.

"What do you want to be when you grow up, kid?" he'd asked me that night, rolling the dice.

"A barmaid in Daytona Beach," I said, attempting to be gangster-like, hoping for his approval.

"You want to be a lawyer, right?" he said, pouring more whiskey. "Have people pay you, not for a lousy dining set but for your advice. Promise me you'll do that."

"I promise," I'd said.

"It's the best return on the money. See, I pay eight hundred dollars for a couch and love seat and sell it for sixteen hundred, right? Well, someone sits down with you and you tell him some bullshit, and—bam!—you make that in a couple hours. I think four hundred dollars an hour is the going rate. It's one-hundred-percent return, and it doesn't cost you nothing but lip service."

"Makes sense," I said, but I knew even then that I'd make a terrible lawyer.

He wasn't going to quit until he beat me again at backgammon. Then he'd be the current reigning champ and we could call it a night.

"Jesus Christ," he said once the liquor had set in, and he slouched in the orange corduroy chair. "Those bastards are

gonna put me out on the street." He meant the loan sharks.
They were the monsters under the bed. I grew up knowing how
much money we had to come up with so they didn't take our
house. Every time, miraculously, he found the funds.
After he finally won and polished off the Jim Beam, he
seemed to doze, his eyes half closed, so I kept quiet and
prayed he'd fall asleep. But then suddenly he started to sob.
He opened his eyes wide. "I can't do it anymore, Lyd. I can't.
I want to die."

I went over to him, kissed his head, and watched his stream
of tears lit by the brightness of the snow from the window.
"You're a winner, Dad. You've always been a winner." I held
him tight. He breathed out, sighing, "I love you, honey." We
stayed like that a long time. Then his head fell forward and I
knew he was out.

I had to wrestle him onto the couch. I put a blanket over him
and stood above looking at him, understanding that in the real
and practical world, my father was not a good man.

I pulled out the American money from my pocket, the
change from the twenty dollars, and I laid it out gingerly on
the ottoman next to the chair. I pressed the dollars flat with
my hands, imitating my mother smoothing towels from the
laundry. *Your hand is an iron*, she would say. I stacked the change
and made a cup of tea and sat with my father's snoring and the
cash. That's when I vowed to make big money. I remember that
I said it out loud, watching the enormous and beautiful flakes
of snow as they swirled from the roof.

I'm gonna make a shitload of money one day.

Once when I was home sick with pneumonia and my mother
was at the hospital working, I called my dad, crying. He left the
shop to bring me lunch—coconut shrimp and a T-bone with a
side of seafood sauce, in white Styrofoam. It was from Grazie
Italian restaurant, two doors down from our shop, where he
took his twenty-minute lunch every day. He'd walk in, passed
the red velour chairs to the kitchen, and point at which pot
looked best and Carmen would plate it for him. I'm pretty sure

now the place was a Mafia front. The restaurant was always empty, apart from the shady men who devoured bowls of carbonara at the table in the back corner.

Anyway, he brought me a movie that day too. *The Verdict* with Paul Newman. The VCR was a relatively new and thrilling thing back then, and I was shocked he found his way around Blockbuster. I imagine he'd slipped the guy twenty bucks instead of going through all the paperwork and showing his driver's license. But what I understood and maybe hadn't until then was that my father loved me. He said my name with such tenderness, cutting up my steak: "Gotta eat this in tiny bites with a sore throat, Lyd."

When the thugs from the bank showed up to change the locks on the chalet, my father laughed. Lou was with us, an entrepreneur even at seventeen, and Lou pleaded like an attorney and bought my dad more time. Lou adored my father and we'd spent every weekend at the chalet, the most magical time of my life, if I think about it. And recently I have. He and my dad kept in touch, always talking shop, long after we broke up.

I know now that the chalet was a lost gem. The town of Salamanca was an Indian reservation, about ten miles from the slopes, and it backed up to the woods and a lovely stream and rolling hills. Deer ate from the lawn and the bird life was remarkable. The fancy ski-resort types paid fortunes for tiny, proper houses in town, where taxes were high.

I broke up with Lou soon after we lost the chalet. I think now it was just too much disappointment to handle, so I went off to study finance at McGill in Montreal, about as far away as I could muster on scholarship money. I didn't come home for four years or answer pleading calls from Lou. He took his broken heart to Geneva, made a fortune as the idea man behind those *AutoTrader* magazines, with franchises worldwide, one of the richest men to come out of Canada, my dad liked to say.

Thirty years on, and I'm a single mom raising two boys. My ex and I are both executives at Union Trust; but he's transferred to another branch since the divorce. He sees the boys on week-ends, and mostly I wonder if I've taken all the wrong paths to keep a shopworn pledge to myself.

I let voice mail pick up when my sister called: I knew it was about Dad. Canada Revenue was after him, she said; he had unpaid taxes for the past decade. He had three days to come up with the money or they'd close the doors to the furniture store. Again.

The thing is, I'm thinking of this trip from long ago, and the tears won't stop. I take quick, panting breaths and exhale to the count of four, like my therapist, Shelley, taught me.

Pretend I'm your father, Shelley advised.

I need to borrow money, honey.

Now you pretend to pick up the phone and tell him.

Say it. No, Dad, I can't give you any more money.

Lydia, say it. Lydia.

I was never any good at role-playing.

I can barely let a week pass without calling him.

"Hi, honey," my dad says, all excited when he hears it's me. "I'm going to move my shop. Forget these goons I'm leasing from."

"Dad, tell me you're downsizing?" I smash a curled fist on the counter. "Goddamn it," I say, but he doesn't hear me.

"New place has three floors, an old-fashioned elevator, and huge windows. This is big-time."

"Dad, you're eighty-two. Isn't it time to stop? You can't scam the government."

"These guys are excited about me coming in, Lyd. Imagine that," he says. "I'm helping revitalize this old part of downtown."

I start to believe it's possible that he has miraculously pulled himself out of another one.

"I'm applying for a municipal grant. They'll offer me twenty-five thousand dollars. I'll get a huge sign and fix it up nice inside. It's got an atrium and everything, honey."

I have never been able to resist the zest in his voice, his ability to make gold out of shit.

"How are you feeling, Dad? How are your knees?"

"Great. How are your knees?"

"Great." In truth, mine had become a little arthritic, and after a neighborhood bike ride with my younger son, they'd swelled like melons.

"I'm taking four thousand grams of vitamin E. It's like adding oil to the Tin Man."

"Listen, we all think you need to slow down. You've got Page to think about." His remarriage at seventy to a thirty-six-year-old dental hygienist was hard, but now none of us resents the fact that we have a young stepmother, and we try to keep her in the fold as best we can.

"Retirement is for schoolteachers," he says, and I could have mouthed those words.

"Guess who I called, Lyd? Your buddy." Immediately I know. "The guy's in Paris. He says, Whaddaya need, Matt-cat? The guy's all class."

"Lucky you've got good-looking children" is what I say, and part of me wants to laugh. Incredible, this guy, my father, who has made so many deals with the devil and is still fighting, still scheming.

"I can't believe you." I'm laughing now. He called Lou. The man I broke, the man who broke me. The one who'd walk a thousand miles across broken glass for me. And I ended it.

"How much do you need, Dad?"

"I'm carrying around this piece of paper to all the banks that says he'll cosign for me," my father says.

I laugh again. I can't do anything else. Lou always said my father reminded him of Willy Loman with a sense of humor. To Lou, twenty grand must be like twenty bucks, but Jesus Christ.

"Dad, you're unbelievable." What nerve to chase down Lou. "I'm a banker, remember. What do you need?" He laughs and tells me he loves me and he has it all taken care of.

I hang up the phone and feel the smallness of my life in this Toronto suburb. I worry about an email I sent another mom at my son's middle school asking her to take Gus to hockey again because I have a meeting. My stomach hurt over inconveniencing the other mom; it makes me feel I'm a bad mother for shirking my taxi duties once again.

I think about my father and the fact that he has called Lou, something I'd been wanting to do since David walked out last year, but I couldn't come up with the courage. I can only chuckle to myself, feeling inspired by the cheekiness of my father, and I wish, even knowing the wish is insane, that I could be more like him.

BREAD

Walking home from the clinic, I repeat the words: *with child, with child*. I say it like I understand what is happening to me. The way I feel, the fright I feel, sinks into me. I could just as easily be talking about the state of this broken country—Kenya—or this town—Kisumu: the disease, the deaths, the mothers I see stealing from their own starving children. But something begins to change in my heart.

The whole time I have been here, such a long time, everything has been happening ahead of me. I've learned not to think. I spend my days keeping up with the next task and fall into my cot exhausted at nightfall. I've preferred it this way. If I am moving, I am doing something—cooking, teaching, cleaning, caring for the children.

You don't waste time worrying about trouble. You rush over to the woman eating her child's bread and tear a piece off for the child. You dig into the parched earth and sow seeds, in the hopes that a green sprout will rise and need tending to. You walk to the one clinic and hope they give you antimalarials and other medicines that are so desperately needed.

But this is all a wing and a prayer of me thinking I know what's best. I don't. Anyway, earlier today, I was at the clinic, a small cement structure with dirty walls. It was crowded with people in pain and people begging for help. The locals here don't have the money for what they need but they come and beg; I help if I can, knowing it's their only chance. The wait was incredibly long, and usually I let the screaming and terrified ahead of me, to plead their cases but today I was there for me.

I looked straight ahead and waited my turn. I went behind the string of brightly colored kangas that sheltered an area for privacy; I squatted and peed into a scratched plastic drinking cup. The young woman, young enough to be my daughter, was the one who told me. She came up to me with cup in hand, her arm touched mine. She said, "You're having a baby, miss."

I'm surprised to find that I feel happy. Everything around me is livelier on this walk, the browns more vivid, the sorrow in the faces I pass on this dirt road seem less desperate somehow. I look down and feel my belly pushing against my cotton dress. I wonder if I'm glowing. I almost laugh out loud thinking of it. I've looked in a mirror only once since we arrived here almost two years ago. I haven't seen myself in so long, because there's nowhere to look. The floors are concrete and the toilet flushes with a pail of old water tossed in. Iron bars stripe every window; there is no glass, and it's another way we aren't able to reflect. No, I've had zero interest in my physical self anyway, only its function. My arms and legs are the parts I check in with. If they work, then I keep going.

The Pillars of Hope orphanage felt like who we were—Stewart and me. We came here together, initially to teach the children (well, we came initially as lovers—two eager, naive people wanting to help: an American and me, a Canadian, in love). We were so content then, arriving to nineteen orphans, with no ostensible sign that they'd been looked after. There was no area set up for teaching, no books, and no desks or chairs.

We created rooms with large rectangles drawn in dirt under the tin roof. We'd sit under what we generously call our patio—a rusted metal awning shading us from the heat. We made ourselves comfortable beside the cooker with the two vats of water, one for flushing toilets and one for preparing food.

We had ideas about what we'd do, how we'd make a difference—I'd teach English and history, he'd teach math and art. We were fools. We pretended there was some structure; we set schedules and lined the children up in rows, but structure has no business here. Teaching the difference between a transitive and intransitive verb? To what end? It was painfully obvious in a matter of days that there was no need for that kind of knowledge, not in conditions that made survival the only consideration. Together we shifted our hopes and lowered our expectations to the ground. What we do all day is try to keep the horror of what is going on around us from getting over the fence. Literally. There is an electric fence above the brick wall surrounding Pillars of Hope and a guard watching every night. Mostly we work hard—cleaning, cooking, marketing, and caring for the children who are often ill with malaria. That is where our energy goes. We talk a lot with the children, but not about what has killed so many of their family members. Their future is bleak, and they know it. Love is the only real thing we can offer. Stewart and I have become good at this, while our own relationship looks less like love every day.

The children have taught us to be more present. They've shared their music, and we dance to their beautiful rhythms every day. A few of the boys beat drums. We move our bodies in the sweet freedom of their voices—angels, all of them. When we're all singing and dancing together it feels as though hope is a possibility. There is an unnamed buzz between us that makes us believe safety and goodness are in reach.

Making believe helps too. My made-up lessons in French have turned into an acting class. I've given each of the children a French name—Pierre, Josée, Phillippe, Jacqueline, and so on, and we wax on in forced French accents with exaggerated hand and body gestures. We keep up the joke, calling each other by our French names. "*Bonjour*, Monique," I'll say chopping greens, and Monique/Irene will say, "*Quelle surprise*, Madame Tremblay," and put the back of her hand up to her head and swing her hips. We have a good laugh. We imagine shopping jaunts on the Champs-Élysées or boat rides along the Seine. I tell them embellished stories of the years I spent in Provence. These fantasies transport them, and Stewart and me too.

Often the gates to the orphanage will open and distant relatives arrive, always wanting something. One man wanted to sell his great-niece for sex; an old Kikuyu woman wanted to take her granddaughter for circumcision; still another man believed he had the right to give his brother's stepchild as a slave to a rich uncle.

They never tell us their reasons, but Pepper, the Luo man who runs the orphanage, finds out. There is little we can do— and it is always the girls they want. We protest and hide the child while Pepper tries to reason with them in Luo. We call the police, who arrive a few days later, if at all. We've lost four girls this way, and saved one. Stewart and I fought about the money we handed over, but we were able to buy Irene back, at least until she turns eighteen next year and is forced out of the orphanage again because of her age.

It's hard to say when it began, but with all the tragedies dropping like bombs around us, Stewart and I slipped into fights. Mrs. Chandra—a short, powerful Indian woman who adopted us while we were in her husband's hardware store buying jembes for digging—takes us in her pickup weekly to deliver food to the rural areas, gifts from the Indian community. Stewart stopped coming weeks ago. He hated the embarrassment of fighting in front of Mrs. C.

Here we were in the pit of one of the worst pandemics in history, and we were squabbling over who forgot to pack the water bottles or how one of us wasn't appreciative enough of the other for some damn detail.

I caught a glimpse of myself in Mrs. Chandra's rearview mirror one day. I was in the back and my face looked hollow, adrift—a sheet of tanned skin with two stones for eyes. I had no notion what I might say to the woman in that mirror if I met her on the street. I think I'd be afraid.

Mrs. Chandra saw the look on my face and said, "Eat something. Bite some bread. You look like a ghost."

With child.

It is so sweetly strange for me to recognize this new situation as a part of who I will be from this day on—a woman who is pregnant, then a mother. Mother. I have not yet come to what I will be. The pregnancy is more foreign to me than this African city that has become my home.

A child. Stewart's child. I have to find him.

But I am thinking of other things—the drugs to bring the children, and how I must hurry to chop the sikuma wiki, sort and soak the beans, and I must talk to young William, who hasn't watered or tended the garden in over a week. I feel like a woman with a burden now, like all the women of Kisumu. It's the women who work, the unspoken rule of this culture. The men wear suits with white pressed shirts that never get soiled, while their wives and sisters and daughters are in rags and worked to the bone.

Mrs. Chandra encouraged us to plant the courtyard with tomatoes, cassava, potatoes, and greens. It was our plan to have the children grow their own food. It seemed like an easy solution.

Oh, to be that naive again.

William was put in charge. Stewart and I picked him out as our star the first day. The boy can talk about the pandemic and get angry, despairing about the future of his country and his life. He has clarity and humor, and even on the worst days he can be lighthearted and confident.

Yet every morning and every afternoon, instead of watering and weeding, he is down at the corner with his gang, boys we don't know. I say *corner*, but it is really just a mark in the road, where one dirt road ends and the bend of another begins. There is a leaning and rusty chain-link fence, a short stretch of it, just beyond the road that at one time may have held back cattle, but it's desiccated land now, without any growth or green. There is a swell of rubbish—Coke bottles, candy wrappers, rusty tin cans, and plastic bags—coming up from a small ditch in front of the fence.

That's where they meet and I know I'll find him there. He'll be loitering to the left of the garbage with the others. They'll be sitting on the hard earth or on the flip side of a washbasin or a flimsy cardboard box if it's handy. Sitting and chewing miraa, and they get high from the leaves.

Very few cars are on the streets, it's mostly hearses of women on foot carrying a coffin above their heads. One in three dies each day here. No one pays much attention to the dead anymore, even as they pass by on a stretcher on their way to being buried. I still look up every time and if I remember I say a silent prayer, but death haunts me less now too. I no longer wake up in the night crying out in fear. I focus on not losing any more of our children, and I keep walking.

I think of Stewart and how good he is with the kids at Pillars, reciting Shakespeare lines he knows by heart and telling plotlines from movies and TV sitcoms they'll never see. I get a flutter in my stomach; I want to tell him the news. He carves puppets, too, from the wood he finds on his walks to town. He carves late at night sitting by candlelight in the courtyard while I sleep.

The fact is, he often can't sleep; he's more anxious and disheartened about each day's grief. Also, he agonizes about us. He talks about holding a puppet show for my thirty-second birthday in August, a production about AIDS. Pepper won't allow us to talk about it openly though, so we sneak it in with the kids wherever we can.

"God will take care of them," Pepper tells us. "It isn't right to interfere."

With child. My pretty secret. I feel happier every minute, and the feeling is a surprise—it makes me see how much I have been living on the other side of happiness. I see William, and my focus turns back to the matter at hand: getting him to understand that responsibility is serious, that it's worth respecting, and that it can bring purpose when there's nothing else. He has become my example, and I am single-minded in my drive to make him perform.

In my mind I see that image of William, smiling, promising me, seemingly sincere, and yet the vegetable sprouts are nearly uprooted from the lack of moisture. He's my favorite, and he lies to me at every turn. The other kids can't see past their belief that prayer will save them, that God will make it all go away. If I were them, I'd want to believe too.

I make my way toward him but I want nothing more than to lie down, to lie with the gladness and the hope. As I walk up to William and his friends, Pepper arrives on his bicycle. Pepper found us, Stewart and me, we were having a picnic on the beach at Mombasa. He told us very little about the orphanage just that they were desperate for help. Stewart and I were just starting to get on each other's nerves then, and we knew it was our chance. "This is our gift to each other," Stewart said. We traveled with Pepper for four days and three nights on rickety buses and crammed matatus across the country to get to this town on the edge of Lake Victoria.

Like Pepper, most of the children are Luo, the gentle tribe. Pepper works hard and expects the same work ethic and kindness from the children too. And yet he gets distracted in his care for them.

"What idle work are you doing, William?" Pepper asks.

William cracks a smile. "I'm waiting."

"You're always waiting. Waiting for no good."

Pepper approaches me and shakes his head. He is angry; he never uses such strong words. This "waiting" seems to be a Kenyan phenomenon. It's the excuse for everything. We used to laugh about it in our first weeks with Pepper, over a Tusker beer split three ways and a plate of rice and beans. "Sitting around, looking around," Stewart would say. "All day long, sitting around, looking around."

"I know exactly what they're waiting for," I would say to him. But that was then.

"Come with me," I tell William now.

When he looks at me, the whites of his eyes are like milk after cereal has been sitting in it too long—a gray-white. The whole time I am thinking of Stewart and this news I have. We decided it would be best if we separated for a while. Everything requires effort now. We can't agree on anything—not even what we will eat or drink or where to sit.

Most days he goes to St. Jude's orphanage on foot, two miles away, a home for juvenile delinquents. A place much worse than here. He and the English guy who run it get on well. He comes back in the late evenings. I wonder about his nights, but I don't ask him as he slides in next to me on the mattress. The children miss him on those days. But today, my clinic day, he will finish around noon, and come back to be with the children in my absence.

Standing over William now, I count slowly to ten in my head. I need to catch my breath, and I know it will take him this long to get up, showing his friends what little regard he has for me, at the same time not wanting me to go off without him. Pepper scowls and pedals away on his bike, having reached his limit. He is one of the few Africans I've seen who are incapable of relaxing. He pedals without letting his bum touch the seat. He is rushing off to see his wife and his children—he has six.

He won't be gone long, though; he is never far from Pillars of Hope.

"How was your day, Akinye?" The children call me that sometimes; it's my Swahili name; it means "big sister." It's a strange swap: foreigners get African names, and the Africans take English—or French—names.

But William is trying to charm me. He knows I like to be called this; it makes me feel a part of them. Also, I can sense that he sees something has changed about me. "The Peace Corps is setting up a temporary prevention center in town. They're testing a new antimalaria drug," I say. "They'll give six months' supply for one dollar a person."

I am thinking of my belly when I say this. In six months I'll be big as a house. A thrill goes through me, anticipation and fear in equal measure.

"Onyango can buy them. No problem," William says, smiling. Onyango is Stewart. *Onyango*, because he is male and because he's a mzungu (white male). Even to people who know us well, our white skin stands for cash. What's below our surface comes as a secondary understanding of who we are.

Everyone loves Onyango. It doesn't help that last week he bought each of the children a bottle of Coke. A full bottle, not a half bottle as we've done before on special occasions. I wouldn't talk to him for days afterward. But I was already not talking to him for something else.

And here I am, standing with William, trying hard for a moment to think of a time when there was any peace between Stewart and me. And William seems to see this too. He is looking down at his hands and smiling. "It is complicated," he says, putting the accent on the last syllable of the word. "Is it not, Akinye?"

"Onyango cannot buy the antimalarials," I say to him. "We could sell our vegetables in the market, William. We could raise the money ourselves. Oh, wait—the garden is all dried up."

William feigns a worried look, pretending that he cares.

I go on. "It rained last week. The vats are full, and the plants are only half-dead."

"I will do it. I will. No trouble, Akinye." He is more silver tongued than he is ambitious. "You are looking tired, Akinye. You should rest. I will take care of everything."

I *am* tired, and his recognition of it makes me want to tell him why. "Get water from one place to another, William," I say.

"I will make you chai with three scoops of sugar when we get back. So sweet." Like coffee, sugar is precious, and it's meant only for Stewart and me and Pepper's friends when they come to visit. We keep a small tin of it hidden in Pepper's safe, along with the Bible.

William gives me a pat on the arm and heads into the little whitewashed building. Eighteen of us live here, from Peter, who is two, up to William and Irene, who are seventeen. There are six rooms; the boys are jammed together in rickety iron beds that line the walls of two rooms, and the girls have a less organized setup.

Stewart and I sleep on a thin mattress in Pepper's room, and we roll it up each morning. All the walls are the same brown, like mocha, but a soiled mocha. Once I walked down to Mr. Chandra's shop alone and bought a can of pistachio-colored paint, my favorite color, thinking the children would be delight-

ed with the brightness of it and the change of task—painting.
But it didn't make a whit of difference to them. The walls are
still half-painted.

I watch William as he opens the iron gate; two of the young
boys, Christian and Paul, chase each other around a dead tire. A
few girls wring out the cleaned clothes and lay them flat against
the concrete to dry. Everyone seems to revive at the sight of
William. He'll probably nap now. It's four o'clock, but the sun
is still very hot.

Without thinking, I go over to the massive bins and fill two
buckets with water and carry them to the garden. I have to
come up with something good. Something good for the father
of this child. Something good about all of this. I have to make
him understand how happy I am about it, what a glad thing it
will be for us.

Rest is what the baby needs, but I don't let myself think of
this. My sleep has been so knotted and daunting lately. It comes
in waves, and often I slip into some mad hallucination about my
family: my sister Kate being held up in a convenience store; my
mother being torn away from my father's empty coffin. None
of these things has happened. I have spent nights chasing after
these apparitions. I wake trembling and Stewart lights a candle
on the ground beside us and holds me for a while, singing Sina-
tra's "Sleep Warm." Sometimes we listen to soft classical music,
with an earphone each from his Walkman. Mozart's Clarinet
Quintet, the only CD we own.

That is a good thing to remember. There is goodness in the
world. Generosity too.

But other memories sneak in.

"I'm no longer part of this," I said to him recently after so
many months of rough edges between us.

"You don't know what love is."

"I'm going to be a crazy person if we don't stop throwing
hate at each other. That's all I know."

"I'm on my way out the door," he said. "No one to watch
over you now."

I thought he said it to scare me. I went on with my tasks; I didn't have time for anything else. There had been mumbled talk of the Red Cross and his desire to work for them again, to have a proper job, not one from a guy we met on a beach; no one had to sign on the dotted line to find orphan work in Kenya. But Stewart needed companionship, people to hang and joke with and to stay up well into the nights talking. I held it against him. He wanted the feeling that comes from working with expatriates in a foreign place, to feel as if he'd finally done something right.

"The kids will miss you," I'd told him.

This morning before I went to the clinic, he came in from the market with mangoes, avocados, and papaya, and a six-pack of canned beer for our tiny fridge, as if we were celebrating something. He knew I wasn't feeling well. He found me sitting on the floor at the edge of the toilet.

"It's all for you," he said.

Once, during our time here, we took a long weekend, just the two of us. Friends of Stewart's invited us to Eldoret, college friends who were doing malaria research at the university. Eldoret is a similar-sized town to Kisumu, but there was something about it, in all its familiar poverty and chaos, that felt like a small university town back home. It felt the way a hopeful weekend away used to feel. I relaxed a little. We laughed and enjoyed his friends from Washington, talked about movies and books we loved, celebrities, and '80s TV. We made meals and lit candles in the mouths of empty Tusker beer bottles.

It felt like us, the good bits, like when we'd met at the National Gallery when Stewart worked as an assistant curator, and my sister Clare worked at the front desk. I ended up at one of their staff parties, and by the close of the night Stewart and I were making out in my car.

Two months later we decided to quit our jobs and do something with our lives. Stewart always wanted to learn Swahili, and I thought it was so ridiculous as an idea that I went for it. In Eldoret we all got Tarot readings from a Turkish woman, in a cavernous shop next to the hotel. "Keep two or three things going, and you'll be okay," she said to me. "Kenya is good for you. Simple. Take one direction." The woman looked over to Stewart and said, "You have many directions, my friend."

Now I'm watering the cassava and set the pail down, nearly dropping it because I am so weak. I realize all over again that I am carrying someone, a tiny cherry of a person. I go down the hall toward the dark room we share at the far end of the orphanage, and I think he is there. I say his name into the dim space. We haven't resolved what happened at the bakery yesterday. It is still between us, like so many other things.

It was a simple fight. About bread. In the black of an evening, we walked the two miles into town to the mini-mall—we wanted to check email and buy a few provisions. It's meant to look European, but it's badly run-down with a rusty sign and paint peeling like dry skin from the face of the building.

Getting an email from a friend was enough to keep us going for days. On the walk we talked pleasantly about the children. It was an effort for both of us; we were too tired to do the edited version of talk that seemed so necessary now. Then, in the bakery, it got stupid. He wanted the cheap round hunk of bread that the locals eat, the stuff that adds weight to an empty belly. I wanted to splurge on the twisty egg bread.

"It's full of sugar," he said. "You American." He laughed when he said it. We were always joking that with my penchant for fast food, I was more American than he was. I could have said, "It'll put hair on my chest," or something sassy, but that was too hard in the moment.

"I'll take that one," I said, pointing to the sugar-glazed loaf. I gave Dipesh, the Indian owner, the money. We started back along the busy street and didn't speak. I could have made conversation, patched things up, but I chose not to. I could have asked about us, about how to solve it, how to try again. I didn't.

Our feet were brushing against the dry brown earth, dust rising with every step and my arm waving the sourdough loaf as if I were the big boss, a woman with a purpose.

Now, back in our room, I imagine telling him the news, and how I'll say it, and try not to think about the fact that his absence could mean that he isn't coming back. This is a place we have come to—a country far from home, and a foreign way of being with each other. And I have never felt more alone.

"Stewart," I say.

Then I hear a commotion outside and turn to look through to the open hallway leading out to the courtyard. A group of men and women are hauling a litter with something heavy on it; an arm dangles from it, and seeing the whiteness of it, I know it's him. The children are screeching. Pepper is shouting in Swahili.

"Stewart!" I shout as I run out. "Stewart!" My hands reach for my head. I'm screaming. "Stewart!" He isn't moving under the gauzy blanket, and everyone is frantic. I grab hold of the dangling arm and lift it to my face. They place his body on the ground, and I'm hysterical, pushing away the blood from his face and shaking him. He doesn't move. I throw my arms over him and lie across his body. Everyone is talking at me. Pepper is yelling. I am covered in blood.

"A jembe over the head," Pepper says. "A boy hit him. That thief hit him with a shovel. Almighty god."

"He's okay," I say to myself out loud, "he's having a baby." I keep saying this over and over. *He's okay, he's having a baby.* I say it until I can't hear myself anymore. I don't remember being taken to my room, but I know when I wake that I have been sleeping a long time. I get up slowly and walk outside, hoping the reality of what has happened will not be what it is, wishing for the impossible. But it surges over me, the grief, the regret, the senselessness of it, the sorrow.

It happened at St. Jude's. It should have been me. I'm the one who found the place, insisting that we do more. I know how dangerous that place is, and still I let him go. I let it happen. It should have been the two of us against the world. Which one of those boys—which one was it? I'm sure he was trying to work with the dry clay; he gave every child a jembe. Jesus Christ. One of those boys, a teenager, killed Stewart to get the money in his pockets. Forty shillings. That's all he had. Enough to buy a burger and a beer. The rich mzungu.

I move slowly into the courtyard now. Irene and Bridget are snapping the ends from bitter greens at the cooker. Pepper is with a group of the young boys near the broken tree swing. They are praying. I kneel at the foot of the garden, grabbing handfuls of the crumbly earth, then opening my palm and letting the dirt fall away. It is still very warm; the sun is behind clouds. I should be crying, but it doesn't seem natural.

There is a strange sense of calm now, a numbness. I touch my abdomen and think of what is happening there. Stewart will never know. I can feel the children behind me, and I feel comforted by their presence. But Stewart isn't with them. If I turn around, he won't be there.

"Will we go to the fields tomorrow with Mrs. Chandra, Akinye?" It's William standing behind me. He's holding the pail full of water. I don't answer. "It's Wednesday tomorrow. She will need our help," he says.

Stewart always told me I didn't love him enough. And now it is too late, and remorse fills every part of me. I place my hand at the base of my belly and imagine I feel movement there.

With child.

"Okay," I say to William. "We'll go. We'll take the milk and bread to the children. That's what we'll do. It's something we can do."

WHISPER SCREAMING

Everyone said Catalina Island was a magical place, and Sydney thought it might be her best chance to clear her mind, to bring it back to some modicum of normalcy. It was only an hour's boat ride away from Long Beach where they lived.

The Catalina Express was there at the dock when she arrived, the exact image of the majestic ferry her phone called up on Google. She'd promised she'd take her children, Tyler and Desi, on this boat, and she would do it too. Soon. It was a sturdy vessel and once she'd paid and was cruising in the open air she was able to fall into the hope for serenity. She imagined with a fluid sense of calm: birds chirping and flat lines, unobstructed views, miles and miles of goodness in the stretch of sea. She imagined answers, like untied ribbons, bobbing toward the shore.

She'd told her husband, Justin, on Wednesday night that she was going, and he ignored her and called her "fucking crazy." Something struck inside Sydney like a match, and that morning after preschool drop-off, she'd packed her sister Tanya's rucksack and drove away in her Kia. Away from her home, her two kids, and Justin. She made sure to leave the car seats in full view on the front porch.

She reassured herself that she just needed time, twenty-four hours on her own.

She had a decision to make.

At first, it seemed to be the plain-as-the-nose-on-your-face truth that Sydney was a self-centered actress, who'd had her freedom snapped at the Achilles by children. Big whoop. *Postpartum or fucking whatever*, her bestie Andy had said to her. *If you ask me*, he'd added unoriginally, *depression is an American luxury*. So Sydney sucked it up, for years, knowing there was truth in Andy's blabbering and anyway she didn't have a choice in the matter. "Like that game at the fair where you have to hammer the rodent's head for a point. I'm clamping down on my impulsivity."

"Whack-a-mole?" Andy said and laughed.

From the helm of the boat, it looked as if Catalina Island might deliver.

Pulling into the quay, the scenery was astonishing, a picture-perfect postcard. Like the French Riviera or that Cinque Terra place in Italy that Tanya kept telling her had birthed the slow-food cooking movement.

Off the long ramp with the rucksack over one shoulder, Sydney started toward the mainland, and a turquoise structure with *Fish and Frites* painted on the side wall. Once she got nearer she saw that it was all boarded up. She kept walking. Up close, Catalina was scruffy. There was a mangy stretch of beach and a messy boardwalk with outdated tourist shops and a dusty lane for the few pedestrians and golf carts. The hills in the distance appeared neither savage nor refined, as if they couldn't decide which face to show. It was only an hour's boat ride from home, but it was another land in another reality altogether.

The people she passed were not bourgeois holidaymakers, or suburban weekenders, or even millennial partyers. None of the stereotypes seemed to apply. A ruddy-faced lady came alongside her with three dogs: one fat, one tall and brown, and another dirty blond poodle. The lady could just as easily be a banker or a cook at that Frites restaurant. Sydney figured it was only a reflection of her state of mind that this was a place that oddly gave you no *sense* of place.

The wind picked up and she slipped into the first decent-looking café on the path. The dreadlocked hippie ahead of her ordered six black coffees and it seemed clear that they were all for him and he'd drink one after another after another. The Rooibos tea Sydney settled on, wanting to avoid stimulants, was warm and milky. For a moment, outside the café with the sun on her face again, in the invigorating sea air, she felt as if this jarring move to be on her own, to get away from the fire of her life, so to speak, was the right one. Maybe she'd done something good for all of them. The kids and herself. And him too.

Once, before Desi was born, when Tyler was still a baby and napping in the afternoon, she put on her runners and left the house. She walked half a mile to Admiral Park, and when she reached the swings at the empty playground, she thought of what she'd done, leaving her son alone in the house, in his crib. Feeling a sudden rush of panic, she screamed—and realized that only a whisper had come. A whisper-scream. She turned and ran as if she was being chased, down Walnut Avenue, until she reached the house, and she jammed the key in the front door and got herself inside.

The little boy was wrapped in sleep, exactly as she'd left him. Sweaty and shaken, she gasped in relief and sadness, then sobbed, and the baby woke. She nursed him back to sleep, undressed and took a cold shower, then got into her pajamas. She let herself believe it was just a dark dream, and she never told anyone what she'd done.

At times, it felt as though she had to nail her feet down not to do it again. But she did do it again. She'd left her precious ones with her sister, Justin's mom, or any friend who would take them. "Just for an hour? You're a lifesaver," she'd say. She'd never go far, just far enough to collect herself, to sit somewhere, smoke her one cig of the day, think, and cry.

There was this terrible side of herself she hated. And another side she barely gave a nod to. That side was quick to joy and goofiness and blissful adoration of her children. It was the side that relinquished the trajectory of her acting career, and for two years she'd slept in the single bed with both kids while Justin studied for his MBA, alone in the master bedroom. He needed all the lights on and the run of the kitchen, as well as the use of the Keurig coffee machine. That was nothing, she thought.

She understood that she was a good mother and also a person dealing with her own shit. In society, you were not allowed to be both. But it wasn't being a mother itself that caused her pain.

At the end of the gimcrack strip, she checked into a hotel. The Metropole. It had a nondescript lobby, all whites and tans and clean, tile flooring. "Late check-out, please," she said. "Is there a corkscrew and wineglass in the room?" She hadn't brought wine but she wanted to be prepared for whatever the evening brought. She was here to right herself and she had one night to do it.

Justin was so often discouraged with her. "Get a hold of yourself, woman," he'd say, when she was rushing around the bungalow with her usual timbre of skittishness, or she was asking the children something over and over. *Did you pack your hoodie? Did you clean your teeth? Where's the goddamn hoodie?* And she cringed when he said, "Get a hold of yourself, woman." And it made her even more afraid of herself. It made her afraid of the ticking time bomb he thought she was.

As if he had any hold on himself. As if anyone does.

Andy had reassured her: it was the fact that she was a mother in the thick of raising two children. "Listen, I've got buckets of money and live alone eating kale chips and reading French novels every night," he told her. "You'll have a lie-down with comfy pillows in heaven one day." But it wasn't the domestic part of her life that bothered her either.

"Will you need more than one key?" the hotel attendant asked her now.

"Yes," she said, because she had been on automatic family-of-four for so long. At hotels, she and Justin would divide and conquer, a child each—one wanting to go to the science museum and the other to the swimming pool. "I mean no," she added. "It's just me." And it made her suddenly aware that she had done this thing, possibly the worst thing. Another wrong move.

"You left the occupation slot blank," the man said, and it occurred to her that his aura blended with the taupe behind him.

"You don't need that," she said and set her palms firmly against the check-in counter.

"You're supposed to complete the form."

"I'm an actor," she said and winced. She hadn't had a role

in five years, and it'd been months since she'd even glanced at the call sheets. But three weeks ago, Doug, the love of her life, offered her the lead in his short important film called *Utah*. It'd be a massive boon for her career, and he had her by the short hairs, offering it to her.

This was the crux of the decision she was here to make. Should she be in temptation's grasp again? What she and Doug had was dangerous, a passion that seemed incapable of being extinguished. They were "on" every minute and flitted from one project to the next as if they had just discovered morning sex and peanut butter toast in bed.

It wasn't the real world. She'd lost weight, didn't pay bills, and was up all night writing scripts. Doug's love had been like oxygen, and she had been completely dependent on it.

Goddamn immature.

Justin had come along when her tether was about to snap. He was the essence of stability. He'd offered a place of calm with clean white sheets. He was lovable. She needed calm and someone to be lovable. He was Tanya's buddy from the ad agency. "The office manager with ambition," her sister had called him, and he had a delightful sense of humor.

She'd made a good choice with Justin.

In the hotel room she sat on the bed and started dialing, then hung up before the call went through. She had to do this alone. She punched the digits again.

"Doug," she said, and hated that she sounded sheepish.

"Hey, babe." That was it, right there; why did she still let him call her babe?

"I'm on Catalina Island with the script," she said.

"That's the Syd I know," he said, laughing. "I'll be on the next boat."

"I'm loving the part," she told him. "Lila is such a badass. What a cathartic role."

"Sydney, you've forgotten how exceptional you are. Let me come and remind you."

"I'm here to study the part." She hadn't packed the script.

"That's what this time is about," she lied. Even before the bike courier's motor revved out of earshot, she'd had the pages out on the kitchen table, highlighting Lila's lines. She'd had the role down in three hours.

"It would mean riches if you did it. The film won't shine without you."

"Ugh, hardly," she gasped.

"You're alone on that Alcatraz island?"

"I'm having dinner at a place called The Lobster Trap. And you know I won't have the lobster, either."

"I've seen pictures. It's like Corsica on Prozac, isn't it?"

"Maybe."

"Well, get a pedicure or something and let the lines percolate."

"You know nothing about how I function."

"I'll be there in an hour," he said, and paused. "Joking."

"I'd kill you. Do not call me back. I'm working."

She put the room key in her jeans pocket and took the stairs two at a time toward the narrow beach. The island did favor Corsica, and she remembered that time during the *mistral* season when she and Doug rented a scooter off the harbor in Nice. She'd packed only shorts and tees, and after two days she felt as if the wind had made holes in her. They spent days on the wild coast doing bits from *Lear* and drinking Corsican Muscadet. Over lamb stew in the cheap hostels, they shouted scenes into the drunken night.

On this island she was dressed too warm and didn't have a layer to take off. She walked along the boardwalk and up a twisty road that seemed endless. She stopped often to breathe, and she felt incapable of taking in the spectacular views. She turned around and headed back. It was four p.m. and she was no closer to deciding. She missed the kids and wanted to go home.

She ordered an ice water on the patio of The Lobster Trap.

It whirled in her core that Tanya was there at the chain-link fence in her place, waiting for Tyler and Desi at the three o'clock bell. Her sister would walk them home via the park before they holed up in front of the telly, until Justin brought their carry-out supper home. She ached, thinking of their hearty smiles, the laughter in their voices, a constant echo in her mind. It saved her from tipping over completely. *Oh, babies, hold on.* She took out her pack of cigarettes, and with her one gloved hand—always a gloved hand—she withdrew the half-smoked butt. She'd started it on the ferry, taking three systematic drags before carefully extinguishing it. A rule she imposed on herself after she was with Justin. Forced discipline. She had quit cold turkey while pregnant and nursing. She was trying to have the same restraint now. She'd choose one man for the sake of her children. Justin. She was going back to him and she was here to make it stick, in her heart, her mind. She would knead it into the salt of her body.

The server, a tall, dark woman, smiled as she set the menu and the ice water down. Sydney thanked her and sipped the water, then opened her journal and wrote:

Justin: Gratitudes
Tyler and Desi.
Kindness.
Co-parenting.
Liberal-minded.
A good papa.
Friend to all.
Lovely to look at.

The thing is, she wanted more. She, herself. For herself. And not depending on anyone else. She still desired to keep acting, she continued to feel attracted to Doug, and she couldn't do a damn thing about any of it. Even though this part was made for her, she must resist.

"You ready?" the woman asked, staring at her.

"I'll have the grilled cheese," she said.

"Good choice," the server said, taking the menu. "Who needs seafood?" The woman's fingers, long and unpolished, were somehow consoling.

"Do you live here?" Sydney asked her.

"Sure do."

"And?"

"It's some kind of paradise."

"Do you have children?"

"Yep. Two boys. All grown."

"Would you say I'm terrible for leaving mine? The children? I mean, their dad knows."

"Depends what you're here for?" She tops off the water and adds, "Well, he's looking after them, isn't he?"

"My sister is, for the most part. But, yeah, he'll be there."

"And you think you'll solve it on Catalina?"

"Decide if I still love him?" She hadn't known this was a question, until she said it. Why was she getting into it with this stranger? Of course it wasn't about the acting. "The thing is, I'm not the best wife in the world."

"I don't want to hear it."

"Sorry. Just the grilled cheese, then, please."

The woman puts her hands on her hips. "Got through raising my kids, off to college they went, and then I was out of there. Do you want a side of ketchup?"

"No. Thank you." As she spoke the words, something moved at Sydney's shoulder. She turned and there was Doug, close enough to touch.

"Good advice," he said. "Do what your heart tells ya, Sydney."

She opened her mouth to speak, but only a small murmur of protest came out. The server assumed Doug was the one, the husband she'd been talking about, and she turned to leave, as if satisfied she'd witnessed the happy ending of a story.

"You're out of your mind," Sydney said to him. *How the hell.* "What kind of asshole are you?"

He sat down. He hadn't changed—the same blue, blue eyes, the same slanting smile. He'd offered the part over the phone and she'd resisted every opportunity for them to meet.

"You're sexy as ever."

"You're ruining everything," she said.

"I brought you a warm coat. We'll pretend we're in Corsica."

He pulled his chair in close and handed her his leather jacket.

"Instead of doing *Lear*, it'll be *Utah*, and you're the star of the show."

"I'm too warm in this."

"The part is made for you, Syd."

"There'll be others."

"I don't have time to do the whole song and dance we do. Listen, I already told you there's no one on Earth who'll do Lila justice. Come on, we're buds now. I'll respect that."

"I'd be beholden to you?"

"If I can't have you, I can watch you work."

"No temptation there."

"They don't have to know anything about it."

"I'm living the commitment I made to my children. Justin doesn't deserve this."

"Why did you lead me here?"

The sky had gone all wispy, the pretty pink brush of evening descending.

"You drew me the map, Sydney. Here I am."

He took her hand and put it up to the side of his cheek. "Well?"

She couldn't think of a single thing to say.

She simply stared ahead, and gently removed her hand from his face.

HAVE MERCY ON US

For months, Alina had been following Darrell. This morning, when he came out of his ratty apartment looking foul like a cat, Alina was leaning against the hydro pole across the street. She kept still, in her plain blue coat and Costco running shoes, playing *Words with Friends* on her flip phone. She hoped she appeared like a trick of his mind. Was she there, or wasn't she? She imagined her presence created an awful feeling in him that he couldn't escape. Darrell was Claudia's boyfriend, and the reason her daughter was in trouble. Darrell had knocked her up when the girl was only seventeen.

Alina and her beau, Franco, as he liked her to call him, share the biggest responsibility for Claudia's son, Sammy. The boy was asleep in the next room, with the worn stuffed lamb under his chin, and Claudia was out, god knows where.

"Ali," Franco yelled, rescuing Alina from her obsessive thoughts. He wasn't angry; yelling was just how Franco's words came out. Alina had been packaging brownie orders for tomorrow's UPS pickup.

"I'm right here," she said, "not a million miles away." But of course she was a million miles away.

"Come look at this matching stripped sweater with the dungarees." Franco smiled and pointed at the laptop screen. He meant *striped*, not *stripped*, but she no longer corrected his English.

Franco had lived in Scarborough for more than twenty years now. He'd immigrated to Toronto from Berlin when the wall came down. She admired his ability to embrace Canada, similar to the way her father had, when she was a child and they left Warsaw, just the two of them, with only 500 zlotys in her father's pocket. She and Franco were both products of the immigrant dream and they had bonded over the beauty and lifestyle they'd been given in Canada, which neither of them took for granted.

"Size five, you think? Sammy's quite a pudge, eh?" Franco said.

"Where's the kid gonna wear all these clothes, Franco? Anyway, they're called overalls."

"I have a coupon. They cost me almost nothing." Franco was a large man and he loved to buy stylish outfits for the little boy. "I enjoy it, Ali," he'd said. "Just let me have this fun." Their postbox was full of catalogs—Jacadi Paris, H&M Junior, Zara kids, Mimi Mioche. What is all this, she'd ask Franco, and he would pluck the ads from her like treasures.

Alina herself was fifty-two. She was Eastern European, blond, and wore petite clothes, and yet she had sizable hands, which seemed to grow as she aged. If the word avuncular could apply to a woman, it would describe Alina.

In the afternoons she left Franco with Sammy and drove to the Catholic elementary parking lot six blocks away and waited in her Camry for Darrell to show. This was the spot, she'd discovered, where he sold drugs to motor heads. She knew he had a phobia of the supernatural, and day by day, with her haunting presence watching him, she felt she was getting to him. In Alina's mind, it was her responsibility to save her daughter from this man, to make him gone.

Like clockwork, after the deals were done, Darrell, who was sinewy in frame and wore lumberjack clothes, went to Tim Horton's. When he ordered his double-double coffee, Alina was at her booth drinking tea, giving him the evil eye. Without fail, Alina would see the black crow outside the window in her booth and she knew it was her father keeping an eye on her. He had died when Claudia was only three, and ever since he appeared as a black crow and she felt his energy so deeply. No one could tell her the crow was not her father. It was him.

Before he died, her father said, "Now that you have a child, Ali, you will never be free again." How true that was. Family history revolves in a circle, she thought, spinning and repeating itself until the end of time.

Now Alina placed six brownies in cellophane wrap, then sealed the box with a sticker that said, *Alina's Gourmet Treats*. It was similar to assembly-line work, she thought. When the timer dinged, she took out the next batch of brownies, set them atop the stove to cool, and placed six more brownies in a box. She had created the baking business out of thin air, out of necessity, when Claudia was in high school and her depression, or whatever it was, led to late-night ambulance rides to Scarborough General.

It happened like this. One night, Alina had arrived home exhausted from the emergency room. She calmly left a voice mail for her boss, Linda, at the bank, where she'd been a teller. *I quit. I'm sorry. It's what I have to do.* What more was there to say? Then she went to the kitchen cupboard and took down the cocoa. She knew the not-so-difficult secret of making brownies crisp on the outside and chewy on the inside. By sunrise, the counters were a bakery. Alina brought the treats to Claudia and the other psych patients on the fourth floor at visiting hours. The desk ladies, nurses, and doctors were almost like friends due to the number of times Claudia had tried to kill herself.

When Franco, who was the custodian at the hospital—that's how they'd met—said, "I see your name in lights: Alina's Famous Brownies," she took it as kindness, but she also understood that she could make something of it. Franco handed out tiny cartons of two-percent milk to everyone, as if it were champagne. "Best brownies on the planet," he toasted. It was one of Franco's talents, to create a party out of ordinary occurrences.

When Franco retired from the hospital two years ago, he moved in with Alina and continued to scatter his sunshine. Somehow, he made himself smaller than his six-foot-one size in the two-bedroom apartment. It was tight quarters with the four of them. Every Saturday—the only day Claudia took time for her boy—Franco organized an outing for him and Alina. They would take the GO train from Scarborough to a posh neighborhood in Toronto, to explore and sometimes visit a fancy children's clothing shop. Franco had the spirit of a tourist with his TTC subway map and his man-purse flat on his big belly, ready for an adventure.

Franco came up beside her now and helped transfer the gift boxes into the large UPS container stationed at the front door.

"Some people are worth melting for," he said, and laughed to himself, quoting Olaf from the movie *Frozen*, which he'd watched a gazillion times with Sammy. Franco treated the boy like the Prince of Arabia, and he paid half the apartment bills. And yet Claudia called Franco a "fucking weirdo" because she ruled everyone with her darkness.

"At lunch, Sammy was making the dopey face of the sea turtles at the glass window," Franco said, and his big eyes softened. "He laughed so much the milk came out his nose. It was so cute."

"Today? All the way to the zoo you went, Franco?" She couldn't believe it.

He smiled. "You don't hear me tell you things. You went like this." He nodded his head. "Okay, you said. Yes, I took him to the zoo."

"You're lying to me," she said, annoyed, even though she knew Franco's nature and of course he took Sammy downtown and thought nothing of it.

"You make trouble out of velvet, Ali. The boy is asleep dreaming of goats. He had fun petting the little animals today. Okay?" He sighed. "Sammy doesn't have friends."

"I was busy getting supplies." Alina knew she was being uptight and unreasonable with Franco, the way she so often was lately.

She couldn't remember a time when she didn't feel pinched.

"I get cooped up. It's just me and Sammy all day long," Franco said.

"It's not your job to entertain him."

"Ali, you have enough butter and cocoa to make brownies to reach the CN Tower. You can't stop Claudia from anything."

Of course, he knew where she went every morning and every afternoon. When she told him she was going to the YMCA to swim, or to the bank to deposit the checks, she knew that he knew she was lying.

"I'm not worried about Claudia," she said. But of course, it was always about Claudia.

"She's solid. You can shake that girl but there is nothing clanking inside of her," Franco said, because he had the ability to see hope, even in someone as destructive as Claudia. He often talked of Claudia's *fiery personality* as if it were a good thing.

"She has no brains in her head," Alina said out loud, as much to herself as to Franco.

"I beg you not to go tomorrow. If it's a sunny day, we'll take Sammy to see the ducks at the park, the three of us together." He was being tender with her and she wanted to smile at him, and yet her face was incapable of anything but a frown.

"Let me see the *stripped* sweater," she said finally and put a hand on his shoulder. He patted her arm and his touch was soft. She didn't want to fight. She was too tired to fight.

"Don't go tomorrow, Ali." He caressed her face.

There was a sound from the hall just then and the two of them shared a look; it was Claudia. Could they make it to their bedroom without her seeing them? But the girl was in the kitchen in seconds. She tossed her heavy purse on the counter and grabbed a brownie in each hand. Claudia was pretty but Alina saw only the purple under her daughter's eyes and the lack of care she took with her frizzy hair and sloppy clothing. Her appearance seemed to announce that no one loved her, and it broke Alina. Had she not showed her love in every moment, even when she was yelling at her?

"I made pierogies," Alina said, moving to the stove. "I'll heat them for you."

"No, Ma." The girl laughed, a bigger laugh than was necessary, and she took another brownie. Alina could tell she was high with her appetite for sugar and the familiar way her eyes wandered. Was she drunk too?

Never mind.

"Franco took Sammy to the zoo today," Alina said, trying in vain to make Claudia see the truth of the situation and how Franco deserved her respect for the joy he brought her child.

"He's a hero, then?" she said, and picked up a pierogi with her fingers and ate it cold.

"What can you say for yourself? Where have you been?" Alina was getting angry now.

"I went to my therapist, okay, and to see friends."

"Darrell?" She couldn't keep the disgust from her voice.

"He's a good person, Ma," Claudia said, and it was as if a wet hand hit Alina's face. Darrell was the one who gave Claudia the heroin, told her it would cure her sadness. She'd actually called him her savior.

"He's a nothing. He takes from you, and gives what in return?"

"Don't you believe in anything, Ma, besides the nuts and bolts of making food and shitting and paying bills?"

Not really, Alina thought. I don't. "I make food and shit and pay bills, all for you."

And to what end? More and more she was growing tired of it, and afraid. Not of that idiot drug dealer. She was afraid of herself and what she would do to him. Alina felt certain she would have to outlive Claudia somehow, at least until Sammy was grown.

"Stop doing me all these favors. And stop bullying my boyfriend." The girl looked so drawn. "You've freaked him out."

"He believes in the devil."

"Aren't you getting tired, Ma? Aren't you sick of your own game?"

She was tired, she had just admitted it to herself, but she would never say it out loud. Maybe because she was an immigrant, and she was stubborn like an ox. "I protect you and the boy every day of your life," Alina said, and in that moment, she wanted to take her daughter in her arms so badly, she wanted to hold her. Even though she was a grown woman the urge to embrace her would never go away.

"I'm Sammy's mother," Claudia said. "I'm looking after him in my own way." The girl walked out of the kitchen toward her bedroom and Alina followed her. In the doorway she watched her thin, pale daughter. She looked ghostly in the wan light coming in from the streetlamp outside. Claudia took off her ill-fitting jeans, and in her T-shirt and underwear she got in bed next to Sammy and laid her arm over her son's small shape. Alina watched the two of them breathing, and in seconds Claudia seemed to be asleep.

Franco came up behind Alina. "Let's go to bed, Ali. You're falling over."

"I've got orders to finish." Tears rested on her cheeks.

He put his arms around her waist, and she leaned back and the tears fell.

"Asleep, they are both angels," she said wistfully, looking at the mother and son looped together.

Last weekend, Franco added lunch to the weekly adventure, such was his boisterous mood.

"You see, Ali, you get the same food for half price at noon in these places," he said, forking his sixteen-dollar plate of flank steak and fancy potatoes. They ordered a bottle of Kroonenberg each as if they were on holiday. "This plate would be thirty-eight Canadian dollars after dark, and we've enough left for takeaway dinner." His cheeks turned pink when he was happy. That was the thing she envied most; he was content with the way his life had turned out. Franco didn't have money, but he spent what he had on the boy and things that pleased him.

After lunch, they wandered until Franco found his coveted boutique called Advice from a Caterpillar. "I love the weekly quest, don't you, Ali?" He gave her hand a squeeze before heading into the shop alone. She sat on a bench in the sun and admired tiny pink buds emerging from a cherry tree. She loosened her wool scarf and tilted her face to the light. She thought of her wish to be a good grandmother, and her hope to separate Sammy from who his father was. But she could not.

Every time she looked at the child, she felt ugly inside. The boy looked just like his father.

Be grateful, she told herself; she was in a quaint neighborhood in the big city and spring was her favorite time of year. She closed her eyes and savored the taste of beer on her warm lips. She prayed. *Dear Lord, forgive my rage, have mercy on me, a sinner. Have mercy on us, please.*

But too soon she gave way to her bleak thoughts again: she imagined her large hands shaking the life from Darrell. Every last bit of it.

"He didn't rape me, Ma. We were together." Claudia had told her this more than once. "The baby isn't possessed. You're his *bopcia*, Mommy."

His bopcia. This was true. She was the boy's *bopcia*, his Polish grandmother, and she was the one to insist the boy call her this as she had called her own grandmother in Warsaw. Why couldn't she get past her anger and open her heart to let love flow to the child? She was like a faucet without any water. She understood that she was the only one who could turn the handle inside of her and open the tap. But how?

Just then Franco returned, rustling a bag. He displayed his purchases on the bench to show her. "European quality," he said, holding up a tiny paisley-print shirt and tan pants. He was grinning. "How could I resist?" They were small clothes for an innocent child. She marveled at this considerate man and his strangeness and beauty. "Feel how soft." She felt the material of the collared shirt.

"Franco," she said, "you can never resist." He shrugged and laughed, and she laughed too.

His chubby fingers folded the clothes neatly and put them back into the bag. She laughed again watching him. He was peculiar, this bearded man with the sweet face. He sat down beside her and took her hand in his. The afternoon warmth was so pleasant, and they sat this way for a long while in the Saturday calm. Often, she was sure her father must have sent Franco to her.

The next day came and she didn't heed Franco's wish. Just after dawn, she'd finished the orders and put the heavy UPS box on the front porch and left the house, and her father, the black crow, was there, like every morning. The bird squawked and cawed, and he could have been saying, "Nooo, ohhh," then, "Nooo, ohhh" telling her not to go out, but she didn't listen. Instead, she went down the steps.

In line at Tim Hortons, she handed the attendant $1.28 in exact change for her black tea. But Darrell was already there, oddly, at her table, sitting in her booth. She suddenly felt afraid.

"You're loca, Bopcia." he called out to her and snorted. He appeared almost confident.

"Never call me that," she said, not moving. "You think I'm crazy? Good."

To the rest of the patrons in line, it may have appeared as if they were related or had planned to meet at the booth.

"Your daughter is psycho, more cuts on her than a butcher's block." Then he stood, came over to where she was standing, and leaned his shoulder into her, a push. She planted her feet. Not budging. His face was mean, and he pushed her again.

"She's a good girl, you low-life." Alina's voice was loud and people stared at them now. But she met his gaze and held her shoulders straight.

"You're a whack job, just leave us alone," he said, but she was sure his voice had weakened.

"Bad luck will follow you," she hissed at him. In the moment, she wanted to strike him. This is who she had become, an old woman who taunted a man in the Tim Hortons, like an ancient troll. She didn't care. She was getting closer to her goal.

"What do you want from me, you fuckin' crazy?" he said.

She wanted him to feel small, the way he seemed now, and she wanted him in pain.

"I have power over you," she shouted. Her fury was so great, she reached out to slap him, but he grabbed her wrist. She heard gasps. She jerked wildly to get out of his hold. They tussled, and she felt out of breath and out of control. She screamed like a wounded mammal. It was a scene.

Darrell was frightened of her; it was in his eyes.

"She should be locked up!" He pointed at her. "This woman is crazy! Charge her with harassment." Alina kept her fists up. A policeman came between them and arm-locked Darrell until he got his hands behind his back.

She heard "Bopcia! Bopcia!"

It was a child's voice. She looked down and there was the boy, Sammy, her grandson.

My god.

"Bopcia?" He was pulling at her pant leg.

"What are you doing?" she scolded him.

"Come here, Sammy?" Franco was there. He looked at Alina with such sadness and disappointment that it stopped her breath.

"Alina," he said, "you've gone too far."

Then a man, maybe the manager of the donut shop, took hold of her arm roughly and pulled her out the door. There were two more policemen outside, and onlookers making a ruckus. Darrell was not in sight. "I was protecting my child," she yelled at them. Franco and the boy watched in horror as she was handcuffed and put in the back of the police car. She wanted to shout out to them to *go home, Bopcia is okay, everything will be fine,* but instead she yelled at the policemen. "He ruined my daughter's life," she said, then repeated her outrage all the way to the station. "I'm innocent." She had become like a character in one of the cop shows she and Franco liked to watch at night. She kept up her fight, talking and shouting through her fingerprinting and the interview, repeating the same thing: "I was protecting my daughter. It was self-defense."

Finally, they let her go.

On the bus ride home, exhausted and staring out the window to the gray sky, she had a horrible memory of Leo, Claudia's father. She and Leo had had an argument and Claudia was a baby, maybe eighteen months. Leo head-locked Alina and threatened to push her down the apartment stairwell. At the same moment Alina's father opened the door at the bottom of the stairs. He was carrying a plastic Safeway bag filled with tomatoes and zucchini from his garden, and he saw the two of them fighting at the top of the stairs. "Leo," her father had called up, taking in the scene. "Let her go. Now." Leo dropped Alina to the floor and her father went up the stairs calmly and into the kitchen and laid the vegetables on the counter. That afternoon, Leo packed his belongings and left for good. Alina was free of the man. Her father had saved her life and all she wanted was to do the same for her daughter.

"I'll be a good parent like you, Papi," she'd told her father that day, reminding herself that she was raising her child alone, just as he had.

"You're leaps ahead of me, scarbie," he'd said. Scarbie had been his pet name for her.

She wanted to get home and share this memory with Franco. She wanted to tell him what she was thinking, that her intention was only to live up to the promise she'd made to her father. It felt as if she'd unlocked a secret door and found hidden treasure.

When she arrived at the apartment, the front door was open. "Franco, are you there? Sammy?" The place was silent. She went down the long hallway and saw Claudia still asleep through the crack in the bedroom door. Alina's cheeks burned with the panic she felt; her head was throbbing. Had they not made it home?

In the master bedroom she found them, Franco and Sammy on the bed, watching TV.

"Bopcia, Bopcia," the boy said and leapt up to hug her. "Did you go to jail?" He was shouting and jumping up and down on the bed.

"Don't be silly," she said. They were watching *The Three Stooges*. The boy had new pajamas, a T-shirt from the *Frozen* movie, and shorts like the ones Franco was wearing. Franco's T-shirt had the face of Olaf on it.

"Did you get hurt, Bopcia?" The boy's arms were tight around her neck and she allowed herself to hug his small body. She lifted him up and cradled him in her lap at the edge of the bed. His warmth was soothing.

"Tell me about the police car."

"Not now," she said tenderly, looking at Franco with tears clouding her vision, seeing how much he resembled the lovable character on his chest. "You two up to something?"

"No, not us, Alina," Franco said, looking away from her and shaking his head.

"We are twins, Bopcia," the boy said, showing her the sister princesses on his top, one arm still hugging her neck.

"Very cute," she said. But then she addressed Franco. "Have you lost hold of your senses? You left the door wide open."

He shrugged, and then turned up the volume on the television.

Sammy curled into her while they watched TV, and she held him close. She didn't get up to check on Claudia or rush to the computer to check her brownie orders. It was peaceful with the boy in her lap while he laughed at the funny men on the screen. Her grandson. She stayed with the two of them until Franco switched off the TV.

"Now, I'll tell you both about the police car," she said, not letting go of Sammy.

ACKNOWLEDGMENTS:

Thank you to everyone at Regal House Press, especially Jaynie Royal and Pam VanDyk, for their excellent work.

I owe much appreciation to Tom Jenks and Carol Edgarian at *Narrative Magazine* for publishing "How I Became a Banker," and "Bread," to Elizabeth Strout who guest edited at *Ploughshares* where "Long Division" was published, to Jon Peede at *The Virginia Quarterly Review* for "Teacups," to Mitch Wieland at *The Idaho Review* for "Zee House," and finally to Kevin Morgan Watson at *Prime Number Magazine* where "Felt and Left Have the Same Letters" was nominated for a Pushcart Prize.

These stories were written in wide-ranging places—Toronto, Calgary, London, Kisumu, Nice, Memphis, and where I now live in Orange, California. It has been a fierce ride and my heart is full of gratitude for so many people I adore and am indebted to. I'm grateful for my time at the University of Memphis where I studied and fell in love with African American literature; thank you to the Pabari family in Kisumu, Kenya, where I worked; and for my publishing years at Harper Collins in Toronto where I discovered that I was a writer and not a publicist.

Thank you to The Sewanee Writers' Conference for the time to write and the beautiful family memories made there. Thanks also to my friends in Orange and at Chapman University, especially Anna Leahy and Doug Dechow, Joanna Levin and Farrell Warner, Jim and Viki Blaylock, Jim and Lynne Doti, and Daniele Struppa and Lisa Sparks, for their support.

So much gratitude to those who have contributed knowingly or otherwise to this book, among them Susan Conners, Julie Bausch, Denny Bausch, Sandra Ballas, Pippa Browne, Gilles and Lyne Bordos, Lisa David, Maggie Lee, Louise Marburg, Jill McCorkle, Pallas Pigeon, Sharon Reynolds, Elena Stoeva,

Rosemary Sieve, Betsy Anderson, Lisa and Robert Port, Allan and Donnie Wier, Tryphena Yeboah, and in memory of Akka Janssen and Robert Bausch.

For my parents; though they are no longer here, they remain my earth; and for my older siblings, who have always been, and always will be, my sky—Karie, Kathy, Randee, Jay and Jodi. For Emily and Adam Chiles, Amanda Bausch, and all my beloved stepfamily. Finally, for Lila, you are all kindness and my bright joy, I love you, and for Richard, who believed from the start, this is for you, my true love.

BOOK CLUB QUESTIONS

1. Cupolo writes about a retired father who travels to Kenya to try to lure his son back home and in another story from the eyes of an imagined Zora Neale Hurston. How did this varied range of voices affect you as a reader?

2. What emotions did these stories bring up for you?

3. There are a range of locations where the stories take place – Kenya, Greece, rural and urban Canada, and the American deep South—where would you like to travel after reading this book?

4. What similarities do these stories share? How did you find that they tied together? What connecting theme did you perceive?

5. Which story stayed with you the most? Why? Would you like to see it continued into a novel?"